Rabindranath Tagore

1861.5.7 - 1941.8.7

羅賓德拉納特 · 泰戈爾

印度詩人,首位獲得諾貝爾文學獎的亞洲文豪,印度及孟加拉國歌的歌詞作者。出身貴族,文學創作範圍廣大,除詩歌之外,也寫了許多小說、劇本、散文……等,代表作有《新月集》、《漂鳥集》、《吉檀迦利》、《流螢集》、《園丁集》。

鄭振鐸

1898.12.19 - 1958.10.17

生於浙江溫州,原籍福建長樂。作家,文學史家,著名學者,五四運動時,積極提倡新文化運動。他所翻譯的《新月集》與《漂鳥集》是「五四運動」後,以白話文翻譯外國詩歌的經典。

U0049526

Stray Birds
&
The Crescent Moon
by
Rabindranath
Tagore

生如夏花
泰戈爾
新月集＆漂鳥集

羅賓德拉納特・泰戈爾 ——————— 詩
譯 ——————— 鄭振鐸

泰戈爾傳

鄭振鐸

　　許多批評家都說，詩人是「人類的兒童」。因為他們都是天真的，和善的。在現在許多詩人中，羅賓德拉納特・泰戈爾（Rabindranath Tagore）更是一個「孩子的天使」。他的詩正如這個天使天真爛漫的臉；看著他，就知道一切事物的意義，就感到和平，感到安慰，並且知道真正相愛。《泰戈爾的哲學》的作者薩瓦帕利・拉達克里希南（S. Radhakrishnan）說：「泰戈爾著作之流行，之所以能引起全世界人的興趣，一半在於他思想中高超的理想主義，一半在於他作品中文學的莊嚴與美麗。他的著作在現今尤有特殊的價值；因為這個文明世界自經大戰後，已宣告物質主義的破產了。」（參閱《泰戈爾的哲學》第二頁）

　　泰戈爾是彭加爾（Bengal）人。

　　印度是一個「詩之國」，詩就是印度人日常生活的一部分。新生的兒童來到這個世界上所受的一次祝福，就是用韻文唱的。孩子大了，如做了不好的事，他母親必定背誦一首小詩告訴他這種行為的不對。在初等學校里，教了字母之後，學生所上的第一課就是一首詩。許多青年心裡受的最初的教訓就是：「能消除這個艱苦世界恐怖的，就是品嘗詩的甘露與交好的朋友。」許多印度人寫的書，也都是用詩的形式來寫；文法的條規，數學的法則，乃至博物學、醫學、天文學、化學、物理學，都是如此。結婚的時候，唱的是歡愉之詩；死屍火葬的時候，他們對於死人的最後的說話，也是引用印度的詩篇。

在這個「詩之國」裡，產生這個偉大詩人泰戈爾自然是沒有什麼奇怪的。

Nandalall Bose 繪

泰戈爾的生辰是一八六一年五月七日。他的家庭是印度的
望族，他的長輩出了許多名人，他的同輩和晚輩也出了好些哲
學家、藝術家。他自己曾說道：「我小時候所得的大利益，就
是文學與藝術的空氣瀰漫於我們家裡。」他的接待室裡，每天
晚上燈都亮著，客人來往不絕。他的兄弟格南德拉（Ganendra）
在家裡搭起戲台演戲，他的父親迪貝德拉那·泰戈爾
（Dabendranath Tagore）更是當時的天才。泰戈爾在此優越的
環境中成長，偉大的詩才受了不少灌溉，自然是要出芽、生枝，
而且開花、結果。

　　泰戈爾的母親死的很早。他的兒童時代，寂寞而不快樂，
他很少出外到街上，或園林裡去遊玩。離了家塾以後，他進了
本地的東方學校，師範學校，又進了英國人辦的彭加爾學校，
之後又被送到英國學法律。但是對學校裡刻板而無味的生活，
他十分憎惡。無論到哪個學校，都不過一年就退學回家。他父
親了解他的性情，並不強迫他去服從學校裡殘酷而不明瞭兒童
個性的教師，只在家裡請了人教他。

　　但他還有兩個偉大的老師呢！一個是自然，一個是平民。
泰戈爾他自己告訴過我們：自然就是他親愛的同伴；她手裡藏
了許多東西，要他去猜。泰戈爾的猜法真是奇怪！凡是她給他
猜的東西，他沒有不一猜就中的。這是因為他與自然界相處已
久而且很深了，他很小的時候就愛她。他家裡有一棵榕樹，他
少時常到樹下洗澡遊玩，到了後來，他還記得它：

　　「繞纏的樹根從你枝幹上懸下，呵，古老的榕樹呀，你日
夜不動地站著，像一個苦行的人在那裡懺悔，你還記得那個孩

子，他的幻想曾同你的影子一同遊戲嗎？」

後來，恆河的風光，喜馬拉亞山的景色，幾乎無不深深地印在他明澈的心鏡裡。

他與他父親的工人交際得很密切。他在地方上管理父親的農產時，除了帕德馬河，他最好的朋友就是一般農民了。所以他竟成了他們內在精神的表現者。

在泰戈爾二十三歲的時候，他與一名女子結了婚。這個婚姻是理想的快樂結合。等孩子們降臨在他家的時候，他又得了新的老師。《新月集》就是在那時寫的。在世界文學家裡，沒有一本詩集比《新月集》描寫兒童更好而且更美麗、真切的了。母親永久的神祕與美，與孩子之天真，都幽婉溫和地達出了十二分。且看這首〈責備〉：

> 「誰都知道你是十分喜歡糖果的——
> 　這就是他們稱你做貪婪的緣故嗎？
> 　　呀，呸！我們是喜歡你的，
> 　　那麼，他們要叫我們什麼呢」

這段母親對她孩子說的話是如何詼諧而慈愛呀！總之，天真爛漫的兒童世界，教導他不少的真理。

Asit Kumar Haldar 繪，原本是〈開始〉的配圖。

Nandalall Bose 繪，〈家庭〉的配圖。

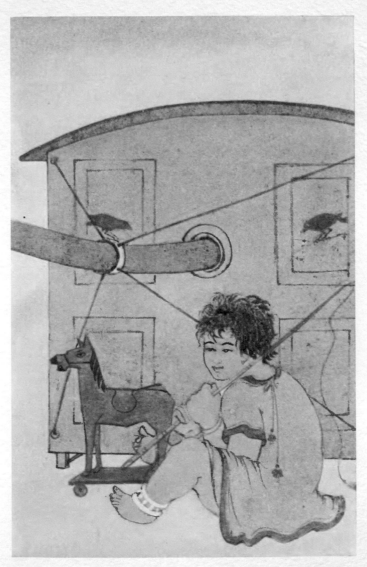

Nandalall Bose 繪，〈英雄〉的配圖。

然而在他三十五歲前後，他的夫人死了。他的愛女、愛兒也都相繼夭亡。

　　這個可怕的陰憂籠罩在他身上，使他寫出世界上最柔和甜美的情歌，使他的靈魂更有力，更尖銳。他的詩，在這個時期也很優美。後來遂轉其筆鋒去做頌神之歌，不復作情詩。

　　「這蔓延的痛苦，因愛與慾望更深邃而成為人類家庭裡的悲哀與快樂，就是永遠融合、流溢在詩人心中發出來的歌聲中的東西了。」

　　這是他《吉檀迦利》（Gitanjali）中的一句，我們讀了覺得他還有餘痛浮繞在筆端呢。

　　一九○二年，他創辦了一個「和平之院」——山鐵尼克當（Shantiniketan）學校，校址離加爾各答不遠。在那個地方，他的兩個大師——自然與兒童——已融合在一起，這個學校的教學法，採用印度的古法，摻以西方的方法，是一種森林學校。凡是到那裡參觀過的人，都認為泰戈爾的計劃非常成功。以前只有二三個學生，現在已經增加到二百人。他得的諾貝爾文學獎金，也捐入此校為基金。聽說，他的著作所得的利益也都消耗在這個學校裡。麥當諾（Macdonald）君做了一篇關於這個「和平之院」的遊記，說：「無論什麼東西在那個地方都是和平、自然而且快活。」任何好爭鬥、好煩惱的成人，一到了這個「和平之院」，聽見早晨兒童清脆抑揚的歌聲，沒有人不忘記他困惱的生之擔負！

　　他的著作多自己譯成英文。最初出版的是《園丁集》。此詩集一出，凡是說英語的民族與懂得英語的民族，無不大為驚訝。以前泰戈爾的名字，除印度外，知道的人極少。自此以後，這個白衣和平天使的威力立刻瀰漫於全人類之間，瑞典的文學會，也立刻把一九一三年的諾貝爾文學獎金，置於他的座前。

一九一五年，他到了日本，受到日本人極狂熱的歡迎。一九二〇年，他到了美國，這個拜金國度的國民也非常鼓舞地去迎接他。一九二一年，他到了德國。德國受歐戰之刺激，思想大變，對於這個東方的「自然之子」，更表示一種特別的敬意。據柏林通信說，他演講的地方，德國人特別布置成森林的景色，因為大家都知道，泰戈爾不僅是「人類的兒童」，而且是「自然的兒童」。

在一九一九年，法郎士、巴比塞、羅素、愛倫開諸人，在法國巴黎發起了「光明社」，提倡永久和平的、非戰的運動，泰戈爾也在其中。他又盡力鼓吹印度的獨立，曾向英國政府請願允許印度的自治，他們竟因此把他的「勳爵」（Sir）頭銜取消。

泰戈爾的文學運動，開始得極早。在他十四歲的時候，已開始編寫劇本。十九歲時，他發表了第一篇小說，因此著名。後來繼續寫了不少劇本，當時即已在彭加爾及加爾各答各劇場演出。到現在，加爾各答還在那裡演出他的戲。

他的著作，初時只在家庭內傳閱，後來才刊登於月刊上。他們同泰戈爾約定，將詩作投稿在此。他的散文著作，最初也登載在同一個雜誌上。

他的著作，最初都是用彭加爾文寫的；凡是說彭加爾話的地方，沒有人不日日歌誦他的詩歌。後來由他自己及朋友將許多詩陸續譯成英文，詩集有《園丁集》、《新月集》、《採果集》、《漂鳥集》、《吉檀迦利》、《愛者之貽與歧路》；劇本有：《犧牲及其他》、《郵局》、《暗室之王》、《春之循環》；論文集有《生之實現》、《人格》、《國家主義》；雜著有《我的回憶》、《餓死及其他》、《家庭與世界》等。

在彭加爾文裡，據印度人說，他的詩較英文寫的更為美麗。一個印度人對葉慈（W. B. Yeats）說：「我每天讀泰戈爾，讀他一行，可以把世上一切的煩惱都忘了。」

他自己也說：

「我的歌坐在你的瞳仁裡。將你的視線，帶入萬物心裡。

我的歌聲，雖因死而沉寂；但是我的詩歌，仍將從你活著的心裡唱出來。」

是的，泰戈爾的歌聲雖有時沉寂，但是只要有人類在世上，他微妙幽婉的詩，仍將永遠由生人的心中唱出來。

詩人泰戈爾的姪子 Abanindranath Tagore 繪，是〈仙人世界〉的配圖。

Surendranath Ganguli 繪，〈紙船〉的配圖。

Surendranath Ganguli 繪，〈商人〉的配圖。

Surendranath Ganguli 繪，〈祝福〉的配圖。

他的戲劇和小說，與詩也有同樣的感化力。一個印度的批評家說：「他的英雄與女英雄都是出於平常人之中，他們淳樸的快樂與憂愁，泰戈爾用異常內在沉刻的情緒，用音樂似的詞句，寫出來給我們看。」

　　就連他的論文，也充溢著詩的趣味與音樂似的詞句。他總歸是一個詩人。

　　「他是我們聖人中的第一個人：不拒絕生命，而能說出生命本質，這就是我們所以愛他的原因。」

　　這是一個印度人的話語。但我們的意見也是如此：

　　我們所以愛他，就是因為他不拒絕生命，而能說出生命的本質。

本文參考書目

（1）K. Roy: R. Tagore: The Man and His Poetry.

（2）R. Tagore: My Reminiscences.

（3）C. Martin: Poets of the Democracy.

（4）W. B. Yeats: Introduction to「Gitanjali」.

（5）"The Crescent Moon" and Other Poeme, by R. Tagore.

文中插圖皆出自 1913 年英文版《新月集》。

目錄

漂鳥集

1

夏天的飛鳥，飛到我的窗前唱歌，又飛去了。

秋天的黃葉，它們沒什麼可唱，只嘆息一聲，飛落在那裡。

Stray birds of summer come to my window to sing and fly away.

And yellow leaves of autumn, which have no songs,

flutter and fall there with a sigh.

2

世界上的一隊小小漂泊者呀，

請留下你們的足印在我的文字裡。

O troupe of little vagrants of the world,

leave your footprints in my words.

3

世界對著它的情人，揭下浩瀚的面具。

它縮小，小如一首歌，小如一枚永恆的吻。

The world puts off its mask of vastness to its lover.

It becomes small as one song, as one kiss of the eternal.

是大地的淚，使她笑靨如花。

It is the tears of the earth that keep her smiles in bloom.

無垠的沙漠熱烈渴求一葉綠草的愛，

綠草搖搖頭，笑著飛開。

The mighty desert is burning for the love of a blade of grass

who shakes her head and laughs and flies away.

如果你為錯過太陽而流淚，那麼你也將錯過群星。

If you shed tears when you miss the sun, you also miss the stars.

7

跳著舞的流水呀，你途經的泥沙，要求著你的歌聲，
你的流動呢。你肯挾跛足的泥沙而俱下麼？

The sands in your way beg for your song and your movement,
dancing water. Will you carry the burden of their lameness?

8

她悵惘的臉，如夜雨般，攪亂我的夢魂。

Her wistful face haunts my dreams like the rain at night.

9

曾經，我們夢見彼此素昧平生。
我們醒來，卻發現我們原是彼此的親愛。

Once we dreamt that we were strangers.
We wake up to find that we were dear to each other.

10

憂思在我的心裡平靜下去，正如暮色降臨在寂靜的山林中。

Sorrow is hushed into peace in my heart
like the evening among the silent trees.

11

那看不見的手指，如慵懶的微風，在我心上奏著潺潺的樂聲。

Some unseen fingers, like idle breeze,
are playing upon my heart the music of the ripples.

12

「海水啊，你在說什麼？」

「永恆的疑問。」

「天空啊，你以什麼回答？」

「永恆的沉默。」

"What language is thine, O sea?"

"The language of eternal question."

"What language is thy answer, O sky?

"The language of eternal silence."

13

靜靜聽呀，我的心，聽那世界的低語，這是它對你的求愛。

Listen, my heart, to the whispers of the world
with which it makes love to you.

14

創造的神秘，有如夜間的黑暗——是偉大的。

而知識的幻影卻不過如晨間之霧。

The mystery of creation is like the darkness of night--it is great.

Delusions of knowledge are like the fog of the morning.

15

不要因為懸崖高聳，便將你的愛置於其上。

Do not seat your love upon a precipice because it is high.

16

今晨，我坐在窗前，世界猶如一個路人，

停留了一會，向我點點頭後離去。

I sit at my window this morning where the world

like a passer-by stops for a moment, nods to me and goes.

17

這些細微的思緒，是樹葉的簌簌之聲；

它們在我心底歡悅地微語。

These little thoughts are the rustle of leaves;

they have their whisper of joy in my mind.

18

你看不見自己，你所見的只是你的影子。

What you are you do not see, what you see is your shadow.

19

神呀，我的那些願望真是愚傻呀，

它們雜在祢的歌聲中喧鬧著呢。

讓我就這麼靜靜聽著吧。

My wishes are fools, they shout across thy songs, my Master.

Let me but listen.

20

我不能選擇最好的。

是最好的選擇我。

I cannot choose the best.

The best chooses me.

21

那些把燈扛在背上的人，將自己的影子投到面前。

They throw their shadows before them who carry their lantern on

their back.

22

我的存在，是一個永久的驚喜，這就是生命。

That I exist is a perpetual surprise which is life.

23

「我們蕭蕭的樹葉發出聲響回答那風和雨。

你又是誰呢，那樣的沉默著？」

「我不過是一朵花。」

"We, the rustling leaves, have a voice that answers the storms,

but who are you so silent?"

"I am a mere flower."

24

休息屬於工作，正如眼瞼屬於眼睛。

Rest belongs to the work as the eyelids to the eyes.

25

人是初生的孩子，他的力量，就是生長的力量。

Man is a born child, his power is the power of growth.

26

神希望我們因祂贈予的鮮花酬答祂，而非因太陽和土地。

God expects answers for the flowers he sends us,

not for the sun and the earth.

27

光明如一個裸體的孩子，快活地在綠葉當中遊戲，

它不知道人是會欺詐的。

The light that plays, like a naked child, among the green leaves

happily knows not that man can lie.

28

美呀，在愛中找尋你自己吧，不要到你鏡子的諂諛去找尋。

O Beauty, find thyself in love, not in the flattery of thy mirror.

29

我的心在全世界的海岸上拍打著她的浪，
以熱淚在上邊寫著她的題記：「我愛你。」

My heart beats her waves at the shore of the world and writes upon
it her signature in tears with the words, "I love thee."

30

「月兒呀，你在等什麼？」
「等著向將取代我的太陽致敬。」

"Moon, for what do you wait?"
"To salute the sun for whom I must make way."

31

綠樹長到我的窗前，仿佛是喑啞的大地發出渴望的聲音。

The trees come up to my window

like the yearning voice of the dumb earth.

32

上帝的清晨，在祂自己看來也是新奇的。

His own mornings are new surprises to God.

33

生命從世界得到資產，愛情使它得到價值。

Life finds its wealth by the claims of the world,

and its worth by the claims of love.

枯竭的河床，並不感謝它的過去。

The dry river-bed finds no thanks for its past.

鳥兒願為一朵雲。

雲兒願為一隻鳥。

The bird wishes it were a cloud.

The cloud wishes it were a bird.

36

瀑布唱道：「我得到自由時便得到了歌。」

The waterfall sings, "I find my song, when I find my freedom."

37

我說不出這顆心為何在沉默中頹喪。

想是為了它那不曾要求、不曾知曉、不曾記得的小小需要。

I cannot tell why this heart languishes in silence.

It is for small needs it never asks, or knows or remembers.

38

姑娘呀，妳在料理家務的時候，肢體歌唱著，

就像山間的溪水歌唱著從小石中流過。

Woman, when you move about in your household

service your limbs sing like a hill stream among its pebbles.

39

當太陽橫過西方的海面時，向著東方它留下最後的敬禮。

The sun goes to cross the Western sea,

leaving its last salutation to the East.

不要因為沒有胃口而責備你的食物。

Do not blame your food because you have no appetite.

群樹如大地的願望般，踮起腳來向天空窺望。

The trees, like the longings of the earth,

stand a-tiptoe to peep at the heaven.

你微微笑，不同我說什麼話。

而我覺得，為此，我已等待良久。

You smiled and talked to me of nothing

and I felt that for this I had been waiting long.

43

水裡的遊魚是沉默的，陸地上的獸是喧鬧的，

空中的飛鳥歌唱著。

但是，人卻兼有海裡的沉默，地上的喧鬧與空中的歌聲。

The fish in the water is silent, the animal on the earth is noisy,

the bird in the air is singing,

But Man has in him the silence of the sea,

the noise of the earth and the music of the air.

44

世界在躊躇的心弦上跑過，奏出憂鬱的樂聲。

The world rushes on over the strings of the lingering heart

making the music of sadness.

45

他把刀劍當作上帝。

當刀劍勝利的時候，他也打敗了自己。

He has made his weapons his gods.

When his weapons win he is defeated himself.

神從創造中找到祂自己。

God finds himself by creating.

陰影戴上她的面紗，秘密地，溫順地，

用她帶著沉默之愛的步伐，尾隨著光。

Shadow, with her veil drawn, follows Light in secret meekness,

with her silent steps of love.

群星不怕自己看著像螢火蟲。

The stars are not afraid to appear like fireflies.

世界對著它的情人，揭下浩瀚的面具．

它縮小，小如一首歌，小如一枚永恆的吻．

The world puts off its mask of vastness to its lover.

It becomes small as one song, as one kiss of the eternal.

49

感謝神，我不是權力之輪，而是被壓在這輪子下的活人之一。

I thank thee that I am none of the wheels of power

but I am one with the living creatures that are crushed by it.

50

心是尖銳的，不是廣博的，它執著在每一處，無法移動。

The mind, sharp but not broad,

sticks at every point but does not move.

51

你的偶像委散在塵土中，這證明，

神即使化為塵土也比你的偶像偉大。

Your idol is shattered in the dust to prove that

God's dust is greater than your idol.

52

人無法在歷史中表現出自己，他在歷史中掙扎著露出頭角。

Man does not reveal himself in his history,

he struggles up through it.

53

玻璃燈因為瓦燈稱它為表親而責備瓦燈。

但明月出來時，玻璃燈卻溫和地微笑，

對明月喊著：「我親愛的，親愛的姊姊。」

While the glass lamp rebukes the earthen for calling it cousin,

the moon rises, and the glass lamp, with a bland smile,

calls her, "My dear, dear sister."

54

如海鷗與波濤相遇，我們相遇了，走近了。

如海鷗飛去，波濤滾滾流開，我們也要分離。

Like the meeting of the seagulls and the waves we meet and come

near. The seagulls fly off, the waves roll away and we depart.

我的白晝已經結束，我像一隻泊在海灘上的小船，
諦聽晚潮舞動的樂聲。

My day is done, and I am like a boat drawn on the beach,
listening to the dance-music of the tide in the evening.

我們的生命是天賦，我們唯有獻出生命，才能得到生命。
Life is given to us; we earn it by giving it.

57

當我們極為謙卑的時候，便是我們極度接近偉大的時候。
We come nearest to the great when we are great in humility.

58

麻雀看見孔雀負擔著它的翎尾，替它擔憂。

The sparrow is sorry for the peacock at the burden of its tail.

59

絕不要害怕那倏忽片刻──永恆之聲這樣唱著。

Never be afraid of the moments--

thus sings the voice of the everlasting.

60

颶風於無路之中尋求最短之路，

又突然在「無有之境」終止了它的追求。

The hurricane seeks the shortest road by the no-road,

and suddenly ends its search in the Nowhere.

在我的杯中，飲了我的酒吧，朋友。

一旦倒在別人的杯裡，這騰跳的酒沫便要消失了。

Take my wine in my own cup, friend.

It loses its wreath of foam when poured into that of others.

「完全」為了對「不全」的愛，把自己裝飾得美麗。

The Perfect decks itself in beauty for the love of the Imperfect.

神對人說：

「我要醫治你，所以傷害你；

要愛你，所以懲罰你。」

God says to man, "I heal you therefore I hurt,

love you therefore punish."

64

感謝火焰給你光明，但是不要忘了執燈的人，

他堅忍地站在黑暗之中。

Thank the flame for its light, but do not forget the lamp holder

standing in the shade with constancy of patience.

65

小草呀，你的足步雖小，但你擁有足下的土地。

Tiny grass, your steps are small,

but you possess the earth under your tread.

66

幼花的蓓蕾綻放了，它叫道：

「親愛的世界呀，請不要萎謝。」

The infant flower opens its bud and cries,

"Dear World, please do not fade."

神厭惡那些偉大的王國，卻絕不會厭惡那小小的花朵。

God grows weary of great kingdoms, but never of little flowers.

錯誤經不起失敗，但是真理可以。

Wrong cannot afford defeat but Right can.

瀑布歌唱道：

「雖然口渴的人只要少許的水，

我依然快活地給了我的全部。」

"I give my whole water in joy,"

sings the waterfall,

"though little of it is enough for the thirsty."

把花朵向上拋擲後無止境的狂歡喜悅，其源泉是哪裡呢？

Where is the fountain that throws up these flowers

in a ceaseless outbreak of ecstasy?

樵夫的斧頭，向樹要斧柄。

樹便給了他。

The woodcutter's axe begged for its handle from the tree.

The tree gave it.

這寡獨的黃昏，罩著霧與雨，在我心孤寂裡，感受它的嘆息。

In my solitude of heart I feel the sigh of this widowed evening

veiled with mist and rain.

73

貞操是從豐富的愛情中生出來的財富。

Chastity is a wealth that comes from abundance of love.

74

霧，像愛情一樣，在山峰的心上遊戲，生出種種美麗的變幻。

The mist, like love, plays upon the heart of the hills

and brings out surprises of beauty.

75

我們錯看世界，反說它欺騙我們。

We read the world wrong and say that it deceives us.

帶著詩魂的風，經過海洋森林，追求它自己的歌聲。

The poet wind is out over the sea and the forest

to seek his own voice.

每一個孩子出生時都捎來訊息：神對人並未灰心失望。

Every child comes with the message that

God is not yet discouraged of man.

綠草尋求地上的伴侶。

樹木尋求天空的寂寞。

The grass seeks her crowd in the earth.

The tree seeks his solitude of the sky.

我們錯看世界，
反說它欺騙我們.

We read the world wrong
and say that it deceives us.

79

人對自己築起心牆。

Man barricades against himself.

80

我的朋友，你的話語飄蕩在我心裡，

像那海水的低吟繚繞在靜聽的松林。

Your voice, my friend, wanders in my heart,

like the muffled sound of the sea among these listening pines.

81

這不可見的暗之火焰，以繁星為其火花，它到底是什麼呢？

What is this unseen flame of darkness whose sparks are the stars?

82

使生如夏花之絢爛，死如秋葉之靜美。

Let life be beautiful like summer flowers

and death like autumn leaves.

83

那些想做好人的，在門外敲著門；愛人的，卻看見門敞開著。

He who wants to do good knocks at the gate;

he who loves finds the gate open.

84

死的時候，眾多和而為一；生的時候，一化為眾多。

神死的時候，宗教便將合而為一。

In death the many becomes one; in life the one becomes many.

Religion will be one when God is dead.

85

藝術家是自然的情人，
所以他是自然的奴隸，也是自然的主人。
The artist is the lover of Nature,
therefore he is her slave and her master.

86

「果實呀，你離我有多遠呢？」
「花呀，我藏在你心底呢。」
"How far are you from me, O Fruit?"
"I am hidden in your heart, O Flower."

87

這份渴望是留給在黑夜裡感覺得到，
白晝裡卻看不見的人。
This longing is for the one who is felt in the dark,
but not seen in the day.

88

露珠對湖水說道：

「你是在荷葉之下的大露珠，

我是在荷葉之上較小的露珠。」

"You are the big drop of dew under the lotus leaf,

I am the smaller one on its upper side,

" said the dewdrop to the lake.

89

刀鞘保護刀的鋒利，並滿足於自己的愚鈍。

The scabbard is content to be dull

when it protects the keenness of the sword.

90

在黑暗中，「一」視如一體；

在光亮中，「一」便視如眾多。

In darkness the One appears as uniform;

in the light the One appears as manifold.

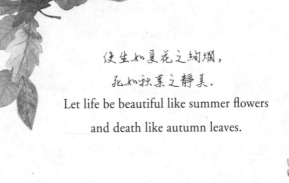

使生如夏花之絢爛，
死如秋葉之靜美．
Let life be beautiful like summer flowers
and death like autumn leaves.

91

大地借助綠草，顯出她自己的殷勤好客。

The great earth makes herself hospitable with the help of the grass.

92

綠葉的生與死乃是旋風的急驟旋轉，

天上繁星間徐緩的轉動則是更廣大的迴旋。

The birth and death of the leaves are the rapid whirls of the eddy

whose wider circles move slowly among stars.

93

權勢對世界說：「妳是我的。」

世界將權勢囚禁在她的寶座之下。

愛情對世界說：「我是妳的。」

世界給予愛情在它屋內來往的自由。

Power said to the world, "You are mine.

The world kept it prisoner on her throne.

Love said to the world, "I am thine."

The world gave it the freedom of her house.

94

濃霧仿佛是大地的願望。

她藏起了太陽，即使那太陽原是她呼求的。

The mist is like the earth's desire.

It hides the sun for whom she cries.

95

安定下來吧，我的心，這些大樹都是祈禱者呀。

Be still, my heart, these great trees are prayers.

96

瞬刻的喧囂，譏笑著永恆的音樂。

The noise of the moment scoffs at the music of the Eternal.

97

我想起許多時代浮泛在生與愛與死之川流上，

這些被遺忘的時代，使我感到離開塵世的自由。

I think of other ages that floated upon the stream of life and love

and death and are forgotten,

and I feel the freedom of passing away.

98

我靈魂裡的憂鬱就是新娘的面紗。

這面紗等著在夜間揭去。

The sadness of my soul is her bride's veil.

It waits to be lifted in the night.

99

死之印記賦予生之硬幣以價值，

使它能夠用生命來購買真正的寶物。

Death's stamp gives value to the coin of life;

making it possible to buy with life what is truly precious.

100

白雲謙遜地站在天之一隅。

晨光為它戴上霞彩。

The cloud stood humbly in a corner of the sky.

The morning crowned it with splendour.

101

塵土受到損辱，卻以花朵來報答。

The dust receives insult and in return offers her flowers.

102

只管走過去，不必逗留著採了花朵來保存，

因為一路上花朵自會繼續開放。

Do not linger to gather flowers to keep them, but walk on,

for flowers will keep themselves blooming all your way.

根是地下的枝。

枝是空中的根。

Roots are the branches down in the earth.

Branches are roots in the air.

遠遠去了的夏之樂音，翱翔於秋日間，尋找它的舊巢。

The music of the far-away summer flutters around the Autumn

seeking its former nest.

不要從你的口袋裡掏出勳績借給你的朋友，這是汙辱他的。

Do not insult your friend by lending him merits

from your own pocket.

106

無名日子的感觸，攀在我心上，
正像那綠色的苔蘚，攀在老樹的周身。

The touch of the nameless days clings to my heart
like mosses round the old tree.

107

回聲嘲笑她的原聲，以證明她是原聲。

The echo mocks her origin to prove she is the original.

108

當富貴利達的人誇說他得到神的特別恩惠時，上帝卻羞慚了。

God is ashamed when the prosperous boasts of His special favour.

109

我投射我自己的影子在我的路上，
因為我有一盞還沒有點起的明燈。

I cast my own shadow upon my path,
because I have a lamp that has not been lighted.

110

人走進喧囂的人群，只為淹沒他沉默的呼喊。

Man goes into the noisy crowd
to drown his own clamour of silence.

111

終止於衰竭的是「死亡」，
但終止於無窮的卻是「圓滿」。

That which ends in exhaustion is death,
but the perfect ending is in the endless.

112

太陽只穿一件樸素的光衣，白雲卻披了燦爛的裙裾。

The sun has his simple robe of light.

The clouds are decked with gorgeousness.

113

山峰如群童之喧嚷，舉起他們的雙臂，想去捉天上的星星。

The hills are like shouts of children who raise their arms,

trying to catch stars.

114

道路雖擁擠卻寂寞，因為它並不被愛。

The road is lonely in its crowd for it is not loved.

115

權勢以惡行自誇，落下的黃葉與浮游的雲朵卻在笑它。

The power that boasts of its mischiefs is laughed at
by the yellow leaves that fall, and clouds that pass by.

116

今天大地在陽光裡向我嚶嚶哼鳴，像織布的婦人，
用一種已忘卻的語言，哼著古代的歌曲。

The earth hums to me today in the sun, like a woman at her
spinng, some ballad of the ancient time in a forgotten tongue.

117

綠草無愧於它所生長的偉大世界。

The grass-blade is worth of the great world where it grows.

118

夢是一個愛談話的妻子。

睡眠是一個默默忍受的丈夫。

Dream is a wife who must talk.

Sleep is a husband who silently suffers.

119

夜與逝去的日子接吻，輕輕在他耳畔說道：「我是死亡，

是你的母親。我將要賦予你嶄新的生命。」

The night kisses the fading day whispering to his ear, "I am

death, your mother. I am to give you fresh birth."

120

黑夜呀，我感覺到你的美了。

你的美如一個將燈熄滅時的可愛女子。

I feel, thy beauty, dark night,

like that of the loved woman when she has put out the lamp.

121

我把那些已逝去世界的繁榮帶到我的世界來。

I carry in my world that flourishes the worlds that have failed.

122

親愛的朋友，好幾次在暮色深沉的黃昏裡，我在這個海岸上，
靜聽著海濤，感受你偉大思想的沉默。

Dear friend, I feel the silence of your great thoughts of may a
deepening eventide on this beach when I listen to these waves.

123

飛鳥以為將魚帶到空中是一種仁慈的舉動。

The bird thinks it is an act of kindness
to give the fish a lift in the air.

124

夜對太陽說道：「在月光裡，你送了情書給我。」

「而我已在綠草上留下淚水作為回答。」

"In the moon thou sendest thy love letters to me,"

said the night to the sun.

"I leave my answers in tears upon the grass."

125

偉人是天生的孩子，

當他死時，便把他偉大的孩提時代給了世界。

The Great is a born child;

when he dies he gives his great childhood to the world.

126

不是槌的打擊，而是水的載歌載舞，使鵝卵石臻於完美。

Not hammerstrokes, but dance of the water

sings the pebbles into perfection.

蜜蜂從花中啜蜜，離開時嚶嚶地道謝。

浮華的蝴蝶卻相信花應該向牠道謝。

Bees sip honey from flowers and hum their thanks when they leave.

The gaudy butterfly is sure that the flowers owe thanks to him.

若你不求說出完全的真理，那麼把真話說出來是很容易的。

To be outspoken is easy when you do not wait

to speak the complete truth.

「可能」問「不可能」：

「你住在什麼地方呢？」

它回答：「在那無能為力之人的夢境裡。」

Asks the Possible to the Impossible,

"Where is your dwelling place?"

"In the dreams of the impotent," comes the answer.

若你把所有的錯誤都關在門外，

真理也要被關在門外面了。

If you shut your door to all errors truth will be shut out.

我聽見我心憂悶之處有聲音在蕭蕭作響

——而我看不見它們。

I hear some rustle of things behind my sadness of heart,

—— I cannot see them.

閒暇在動作時便是工作。

靜止的海水蕩動時便成波濤。

Leisure in its activity is work.

The stillness of the sea stirs in waves.

綠葉戀愛時便成了花。

花崇拜時便結成了果。

The leaf becomes flower when it loves.

The flower becomes fruit when it worships.

埋在地下的樹根使樹枝產生果實，卻不要什麼報酬。

The roots below the earth claim no rewards

for making the branches fruitful.

陰雨的黃昏，風無休止地吹著。

我看著搖曳的樹枝，想念萬物的偉大。

This rainy evening the wind is restless.

I look at the swaying branches and ponder

over the greatness of all things.

子夜的風雨，如一個巨大的孩子，

在不合時宜的黑夜裡醒來，開始遊戲喧鬧。

Storm of midnight, like a giant child awakened

in the untimely dark, has begun to play and shout.

137

海呀，你是這暴風雨的孤寂新婦，

雖掀起波浪追隨你的情人，卻毫無用處。

Thou raisest thy waves vainly to follow thy lover.

O sea, thou lonely bride of the storm.

138

文字對工作說道：「我慚愧於我的虛無。」

工作對文字說道：「我看見你時，便知道自己有多貧乏。」

"I am ashamed of my emptiness," said the Word to the Work.

"I know how poor I am when I see you,"

said the Work to the Word.

綠葉戀愛時便成了花.
花崇拜時便結成了果.

The leaf becomes flower when it loves.

The flower becomes fruit when it worships.

漂鳥集

時間是變化的財富。時鐘模仿它，卻只有變化而無財富。

Time is the wealth of change, but the clock in its parody

makes it mere change and no wealth.

真理穿了衣裳，覺得事實太拘束了。

在想像中，她卻移動得很舒暢。

Truth in her dress finds facts too tight.

In fiction she moves with ease.

當我到此處或彼方旅行時，路呀，我厭倦了你；

但此刻，當你引導我到各處去時，我便愛上你，與你結合。

When I travelled to here and to there, I was tired of thee,

ORoad, but now when thou leadest me

to everywhere I am wedded to thee in love.

讓我設想，在群星之中，

有那麼一顆星引導我的生命通過不可知的黑暗。

Let me think that there is one among those stars that

guides my life through the dark unknown.

姑娘，妳用妳美麗的手指，觸碰著我的器物，

秩序便如音樂般奏了出來。

Woman, with the grace of your fingers you touched my things

and order came out like music.

{144}

一道憂鬱的聲響，築巢於時光的殘骸中。

它在夜裡向我唱道：「我愛你。」

One sad voice has its nest among the ruins of the years.

It sings to me in the night, —— "I loved you."

145

燃燒的火，以它熊熊的光焰警告我不要走近。

把我從潛藏在灰中的餘燼裡解救出來吧。

The flaming fire warns me off by its own glow.

Save me from the dying embers hidden under ashes.

146

我有群星在天上，

但是呀，我屋裡的小燈卻沒有點亮。

I have my stars in the sky,

But oh for my little lamp unlit in my house.

147

死去的文字化為塵土沾上了你。

用沉默洗淨你的靈魂吧。

The dust of the dead words clings to thee.

Wash thy soul with silence.

148

生命裡有許多縫隙，從中透出憂鬱的死亡之音。

Gaps are left in life through which comes the sad music of death.

149

世界在早晨敞開了它的光明之心。

出來吧，我的心，帶著你的愛去與它相會。

The world has opened its heart of light in the morning.

Come out, my heart, with thy love to meet it.

150

我的思想隨著閃耀的綠葉而閃耀；

我的心靈因日光的撫觸而歌唱；

我的生命因為和萬物一同浮泛在空間的蔚藍、

在時間的墨黑而感到歡快。

My thoughts shimmer with these shimmering leaves and my heart

sings with the touch of this sunlight; my life is glad to be floating

with all things into the blue of space, into the dark of time.

神巨大的權威存在於柔和的微風裡，而不在狂風暴雨之中。

God's great power is in the gentle breeze, not in the storm.

152

在夢中，一切都散漫著，都壓著我，但這不過是一場夢呀。

當我醒來時，我將發現萬物盡歸於你，我也便將自由。

This is a dream in which things are all loose and they oppress.

I shall find them gathered in thee when I awake and shall be free.

153

落日問道：「有誰繼續我的職務呢？」

瓦燈回答：「我會盡我所能地做去，我的主人。」

"Who is there to take up my duties?" asked the setting sun.

"I shall do what I can, my Master," said the earthen lamp.

採摘花瓣時，得不到花的美。

By plucking her petals you do not gather the beauty of the flower.

沉默蘊蓄著語聲，正如鳥巢擁圍著睡鳥。

Silence will carry your voice like the nest that
holds the sleeping birds.

偉大不怕渺小的同遊。
中庸卻遠而避之。

The Great walks with the Small without fear.
The Middling keeps aloof.

157

夜祕密地綻放了花，卻讓白日去領受謝意。

The night opens the flowers in secret and allows the day to get thanks.

158

權勢認為犧牲者的痛苦是忘恩負義。

Power takes as ingratitude the writhings of its victims.

159

當我們以滿足為樂時，我們便能與果實愉快的分別。

When we rejoice in our fulness,

then we can part with our fruits with joy.

78

160

雨點吻著大地，微語道：「我們是你思家的孩子，母親，
現在從天上回到你這裡來了。」

The raindrops kissed the earth and whispered,--"We are thy
homesick children, mother, come back to thee from the heaven."

161

蛛網像是要捕捉露滴，卻捉住了蒼蠅。

The cobweb pretends to catch dew-drops and catches flies.

162

愛情呀，當你手拿燃燒的痛苦之燈走來時，我能看清你的臉，
並視你為幸福。

Love! When you come with the burning lamp of pain in your hand,
I can see your face and know you as bliss.

163

螢火蟲對天上的星星說道：
「學者說你的光明總有一天會消滅。」
天上的群星不說話。

"The learned say that your lights will one day be no more."
Said the firefly to the stars.
The stars made no answer.

164

在黃昏的微光裡，有那清晨的鳥兒來到我沉默的巢。
In the dusk of the evening the bird of some early dawn
comes to the nest of my silence.

165

思想掠過我的心上，如一群野鴨飛過天空。
我聽見它們的鼓翼之聲了。
Thoughts pass in my mind like flocks of ducks in the sky.
I hear the voice of their wings.

166

溝洫總喜歡想：河流是為了給它供水而存在。

The canal loves to think that rivers exist solely

to supply it with water.

167

世界以痛楚親吻我的魂魄，卻要我以歌聲做為報答。

The world has kissed my soul with its pain,

asking for its return in songs.

168

壓迫我的，到底是我想要離開的靈魂呢，

還是世界的靈魂敲著我的心門，想要進來呢？

That which oppresses me, is it my soul

trying to come out in the open, or the soul of the world

knocking at my heart for its entrance?

169

思想以自己的語言餵養自己，並成長茁壯。

Thought feeds itself with its own words and grows.

170

我把我的心鉢輕輕浸入這沉默時刻中，它盛滿了愛。

I have dipped the vessel of my heart into this silent hour;

it has filled with love.

171

你或許有工作，也或許沒有。

當你不得不說：「讓我們做點事吧」，那麼胡鬧就要開始了。

Either you have work or you have not.

When you have to say, "Let us do something,"

then begins mischief.

172

向日葵羞於把無名的花朵看作它的同胞。

太陽升起，卻向它微笑，說道：「你好嗎，我親愛的？」

The sunflower blushed to own the nameless flower as her kin.

The sun rose and smiled on it, saying, "Are you well, my darling?"

173

「誰如命運般催著我向前走呢？」

「是我自己，在背後大跨步走著。」

"Who drives me forward like fate?"

"The Myself striding on my back."

174

雲將河流的水杯注滿，自己卻藏在遠山之中。

The clouds fill the watercups of the river,

hiding themselves in the distant hills.

175

我一路走去，我的水瓶一路灑出水來。

只剩下極少極少的水夠我回家使用了。

I spill water from my water jar as I walk on my way,

Very little remains for my home.

176

杯中的水是光輝的；海中的水卻是漆黑的。

微小的道理可以用文字說清，巨大的真理卻只有無限的沉默。

The water in a vessel is sparkling; the water in the sea is dark.

The small truth has words that are clear;

the great truth has great silence.

177

你的微笑是你田園裡的花，你的談吐是你山上的松林蕭蕭；

但是你的心呀，卻是那名我們全都認識的女子。

Your smile was the flowers of your own fields,

your talk was the rustle of your own mountain pines,

but your heart was the woman that we all know.

178

我把小禮物留給我所愛的人——大禮物卻留給所有人。

It is the little things that I leave behind for my loved ones, ——

great things are for everyone.

179

姑娘呀，妳用淚海包容世界的心，正如大海包容大地。

Woman, thou hast encircled the world's heart

with the depth of thy tears as the sea has the earth.

180

太陽以微笑向我問候。

他憂悶的雨滴姊姊，則向我的心談話。

The sunshine greets me with a smile.

The rain, his sad sister, talks to my heart.

181

我的晝間之花，落下它那被遺忘的花瓣。

在黃昏中，這花成熟為一顆記憶的金果。

My flower of the day dropped its petals forgotten.

In the evening it ripens into a golden fruit of memory.

182

我像那夜間之路，正悄悄諦聽記憶的足音。

I am like the road in the night listening

to the footfalls of its memories in silence.

183

黃昏的天空，在我看來，

像一扇窗，一盞燈，像燈火背後的一次等待。

The evening sky to me is

like a window, and a lighted lamp, and a waiting behind it.

86

184

急於做好事的人，反而找不到時間去做好人。

He who is too busy doing good finds no time to be good.

185

我是秋雲，空落落地不承載任何雨水，

但在成熟的稻田中，可以看見我的充盈。

I am the autumn cloud, empty of rain,

see my fulness in the field of ripened rice.

186

他們憎恨，他們殘殺，而人們讚揚他們。

上帝卻羞慚了，匆匆把祂的記憶埋藏在綠草下面。

They hated and killed and men praised them.

But God in shame hastens to hide its memory under the green

grass.

187

腳趾乃是捨棄了過往的手指。

Toes are the fingers that have forsaken their past.

188

黑暗向光明旅行，盲目卻向死亡旅行。

Darkness travels towards light, but blindness towards death.

189

小狗疑心宇宙陰謀篡奪牠的位置。

The pet dog suspects the universe for scheming to take its place.

190

靜靜坐著吧，我的心，不要揚起塵土。

讓世界自己尋路向你走來。

Sit still my heart, do not raise your dust.

Let the world find its way to you.

191

弓在箭要射出之前，低聲對箭說：
「你的自由就是我的自由。」

The bow whispers to the arrow before it speeds forth ——
"Your freedom is mine."

192

姑娘呀，妳的笑聲裡有生命之泉的樂聲。

Woman, in your laughter
you have the music of the fountain of life.

193

只有理智的心，恰如一柄全是鋒刃的刀。
它讓使用它的人手上流血。

A mind all logic is like a knife all blade.
It makes the hand bleed that uses it.

194

神愛人間的燈火甚於祂自己的明星。

God loves man's lamp lights better than his own great stars.

195

這世界原是狂風驟雨，直到美妙的音樂馴服了它。

This world is the world of wild storms kept tame

with the music of beauty.

196

晚霞向太陽說道：

「我的心經過你的親吻，便似金子打成的寶箱了。」

"My heart is like the golden casket of thy kiss,"

said the sunset cloud to the sun.

接觸也許會使你屠戮；遠離也許能讓你佔有。

By touching you may kill, by keeping away you may possess.

蟋蟀的唧唧，夜雨的淅瀝，從黑暗中傳到我的耳邊，

好似我已逝的少年時代簌簌地來到我夢中。

The cricket's chirp and the patter of rain come to me through

the dark, like the rustle of dreams from my past youth.

花朵向星辰落盡的清晨哭喊：「我失去了所有的露珠。」

"I have lost my dewdrop,"

cries the flower to the morning sky that has lost all its stars.

弓在箭要射出之前，

低聲對箭說：

「你的自由就是我的自由。」

The bow whispers to the arrow

before it speeds forth ——

"Your freedom is mine."

200

燃燒的木塊生出熊熊火光，叫道：

「這是我的花朵，我的死亡。」

The burning log bursts in flame and cries, ——

"This is my flower, my death."

201

黃蜂認為鄰蜂儲蜜之巢太小。

牠的鄰人要牠建一個更小的。

The wasp thinks that the honey-hive of the neighbouring bees

is too small.

His neighbours ask him to build one still smaller.

202

河岸向河流說道：「我留不住你的波浪。

讓我留住你的足印在我的心裡吧。」

"I cannot keep your waves," says the bank to the river.

"Let me keep your footprints in my heart."

白日以小小地球的喧擾，淹沒了整個宇宙的沉默。

The day, with the noise of this little earth,

drowns the silence of all worlds.

歌聲在天空中感到無限，圖畫在地上感到無限，然而詩呢，

無論在空中，在地上都是如此。

因為詩的詞句有走動的意義與飛翔的樂音。

The song feels the infinite in the air, the picture in the earth,

the poem in the air and the earth;

For its words have meaning that walks and music that soars.

太陽在西方落下時，屬於早晨的東方已悄悄站在他面前。

When the sun goes down to the West,

the East of his morning stands before him in silence.

206

讓我不要錯誤地將自己放在我的世界裡而使它反對我。

Let me not put myself wrongly to my world and set it against me.

207

榮譽使我感到慚愧，因為我暗地裡渴求著它。

Praise shames me, for I secretly beg for it.

208

當我沒有什麼事做時，便讓我不做任何事，不受騷擾地沉入
安靜深處吧，一如海水沉默時海邊的暮色。

Let my doing nothing when I have nothing to do become
untroubled in its depth of peace like the evening in the seashore
when the water is silent.

209

少女呀，妳的純樸，如湖水之碧，展現出妳深邃的真理。

Maiden, your simplicity, like the blueness of the lake,

reveals your depth of truth.

210

最好的不會獨來，

它伴著一切同來。

The best does not come alone.

It comes with the company of the all.

211

神的右手是慈愛的，但祂的左手卻是可怕的。

God's right hand is gentle, but terrible is his left hand.

212

我的暮色來自陌生的樹林，它的語言我的晨星不懂。

My evening came among the alien trees and spoke in a language

which my morning stars did not know.

213

夜的黑暗是一口布袋，迸出黎明的金光。

Night's darkness is a bag that bursts with the gold of the dawn.

214

我們的欲望把彩虹的顏色借給那不過是縹緲雲霧的人生。

Our desire lends the colours of the rainbow

to the mere mists and vapours of life.

215

神等待著，要從人的手上把祂的花朵作為禮物贏回去。

God waits to win back his own flowers as gifts from man's hands.

216

我的憂思纏繞著我，要問我它自己的名字。

My sad thoughts tease me asking me their own names.

217

果實的作用是珍貴的，花朵的作用是甜美的；

就讓我發揮綠葉的作用吧，

綠葉是謙遜地，專心垂著綠蔭的。

The service of the fruit is precious,

the service of the flower is sweet,

but let my service be the service of the leaves

in its shade of humble devotion.

218

我的心向閒適的風張開了帆，要到無論何處的蔭涼之島去。

My heart has spread its sails to the idle winds

for the shadowy island of Anywhere.

219

一群人是殘暴的，一個人是良善的。

Men are cruel, but Man is kind.

220

讓我做你的杯吧，讓我為了你，而且為了你的人而盛滿水吧。

Make me thy cup and let my fulness be for thee and for thine.

狂風暴雨像某位天神痛苦的的哭聲，

因為祂的愛情被大地所拒絕。

The storm is like the cry of some god in pain

whose love the earth refuses.

世界不會流失，因為死亡並不是一個裂縫。

The world does not leak because death is not a crack.

生命因為付出了愛而更為富足。

Life has become richer by the love that has been lost.

224

我的朋友，你偉大的心閃射出東方朝陽的光芒，

正如黎明中的積雪孤峰。

My friend, your great heart shone with the sunrise of the East

like the snowy summit of a lonely hill in the dawn.

225

死之流泉，使生之止水活躍。

The fountain of death makes the still water of life play.

226

那些有一切東西而沒有您的人，我的上帝，

在譏笑著那些沒有別的東西而只有您的人呢。

Those who have everything but thee, my God,

laugh at those who have nothing but thyself.

227

生命的律動在它自己的樂音裡得到歇息。

The movement of life has its rest in its own music.

228

踢躂只能從地上揚起塵土而不能得到收獲。

Kicks only raise dust and not crops from the earth.

229

我們的名字，便是夜裡海波上發出的光，

痕跡也不留就湮滅了。

Our names are the light that glows on the sea waves at night and

then dies without leaving its signature.

230

讓看見玫瑰的人也看見它的刺。

Let him only see the thorns who has eyes to see the rose.

231

在鳥翼上鑲了金子，鳥便永不能再在天上翱翔。

Set bird's wings with gold and it will never again soar in the sky.

232

我們這處的荷花又在這陌生的水上開了花，

放出同樣的清香，只是名字換了。

The same lotus of our clime blooms here in the alien water

with the same sweetness, under another name.

233

在心的遠景裡，那相隔的距離顯得更遙遠了。

In heart's perspective the distance looms large.

234

月兒把她的光明遍照在天上，卻留下陰影給自己。

The moon has her light all over the sky, her dark spots to herself.

235

不要說「這是早晨」，別用一個來自昨日的名詞把它打發掉。

這是你第一次看到它，把它當作還沒有名字的新生兒吧。

Do not say, "It is morning," and dismiss it

with a name of yesterday.

See it for the first time as a new-born child that has no name.

236

青煙對天空誇口，灰燼對大地誇口，都以為它們是火的兄弟。

Smoke boasts to the sky, and Ashes to the earth,

that they are brothers to the fire.

237

雨滴向茉莉微語：「把我永久留在你心裡吧。」

茉莉嘆息了一聲，落在地上。

The raindrop whispered to the jasmine,

"Keep me in your heart for ever."

The jasmine sighed, "Alas," and dropped to the ground.

膽怯的思想呀，不要怕我。

我是個詩人。

Timid thoughts, do not be afraid of me. I am a poet.

我的心在朦朧的沉默裡，似乎充滿了蟋蟀的鳴聲
——那是聲音的灰暗微光。

The dim silence of my mind seems filled with crickets' chirp

— the grey twilight of sound.

爆竹呀，你對群星的侮蔑，又跟著你回到地上來了。

Rockets, your insult to the stars follows yourself back to the earth.

241

您曾經帶領我，穿過我白天擁擠不堪的旅程，

到達我黃昏的孤寂之境。

在通宵的寂靜裡，我等待著它的意義。

Thou hast led me through my crowded travels of the day

to my evening's loneliness.

I wait for its meaning through the stillness of the night.

242

我們的生命就像渡過一片大海，我們都相聚在這狹小的舟中。

死亡時，我們便靠岸，各往各的世界去。

This life is the crossing of a sea,

where we meet in the same narrow ship.

In death we reach the shore and go to our different worlds.

243

真理之川從它錯誤之溝渠中流過。

The stream of truth flows through its channels of mistakes.

今天我的心想家了，想著那跨越時間之海的甜蜜。

My heart is homesick today for the one sweet hour

across the sea of time.

鳥的歌聲是曙光從大地反響過去的回聲。

The bird-song is the echo of the morning light back from the earth.

晨光問毛茛：「你是驕傲得不肯和我接吻嗎？」

"Are you too proud to kiss me?"

the morning light asks the buttercup.

247

小花問道：「我要如何對你詠唱，如何崇拜你呢，太陽啊？」

太陽答道：「你只要純潔素樸的沉默就可以了。」

"How may I sing to thee and worship, O Sun?"

asked the little flower.

"By the simple silence of thy purity," answered the sun.

248

當人是獸時，他比獸還壞。

Man is worse than an animal when he is an animal.

249

烏雲接受光的親吻便成了天上的花。

Dark clouds become heaven's flowers when kissed by light.

250

不要讓刀鋒譏笑刀柄的拙鈍。

Let not the sword-blade mock its handle for being blunt.

251

夜的沉默，如深深的燈盞，銀河便是它燃著的燈光。

The night's silence, like a deep lamp,

is burning with the light of its milky way.

252

死亡像大海無限的歌聲，日夜衝擊著生命的光明島嶼。

Around the sunny island of Life swells day and night

death's limitless song of the sea.

253

這山豈不就像一朵花嗎？那花瓣似的山峰正啜飲著日光。

Is not this mountain like a flower,

with its petals of hills, drinking the sunlight?

254

「真實」的含義被誤解，輕重被倒置，那就成了「不實」。

The real with its meaning read wrong and

emphasis misplaced is the unreal.

255

我的心呀，從世界的流動中找到你的美吧，

正如那小船得到微風與流水的優雅。

Find your beauty, my heart, from the world's movement, like the

boat that has the grace of the wind and the water.

眼睛不以眼力而以眼鏡為傲。

The eyes are not proud of their sight but of their eyeglasses.

我住在我的小小世界裡，生怕它再縮小一丁點兒。把我抬舉
到您的世界裡去吧，讓我有高高興興失去一切的自由。

I live in this little world of mine and am afraid to make it the least
less. Lift me into thy world and let me have the freedom gladly
to lose my all.

虛偽永遠不會因為它自權力中生長而成為真實。

The false can never grow into truth by growing in power.

259

我的心，同它拍岸的波浪之歌，

渴望著要撫愛這個陽光熙和的綠色世界。

My heart, with its lapping waves of song,

longs to caress this green world of the sunny day.

260

道旁的草，去愛那天上的星吧，

你的夢境便可在花朵裡實現了。

Wayside grass, love the star,

then your dreams will come out in flowers.

261

讓你的音樂如一柄利刃，直刺入市井喧擾的心中。

Let your music, like a sword,

pierce the noise of the market to its heart.

262

這樹的顫動之葉，像一個嬰兒的手指，觸動著我的心。

The trembling leaves of this tree touch my heart
like the fingers of an infant child.

263

我靈魂裡的憂鬱就是新娘的面紗。
這面紗等著在夜間揭去。

The sadness of my soul is her bride's veil.
It waits to be lifted in the night.

264

小花睡在塵土裡。
它尋求蝴蝶走的道路。

The little flower lies in the dust.
It sought the path of the butterfly.

我在道路縱橫的世界上。

夜來了。打開您的門吧，家之世界啊！

I am in the world of the roads. The night comes.

Open thy gate, thou world of the home.

我已經唱過您白天的歌。

黃昏的時候，讓我拿著您的燈走過風雨飄搖的道路吧。

I have sung the songs of thy day.

In the evening let me carry thy lamp through the stormy path.

我不要求你進我的屋裡。

我只求你到我無量的孤寂裡，我的愛人！

I do not ask thee into the house.

Come into my infinite loneliness, my Lover.

268

死亡屬於生命，正與出生一樣。

舉足是走路，正如落足也是。

Death belongs to life as birth does.

The walk is in the raising of the foot as in the laying of it down.

269

我已學會你在花與陽光裡那些微語的意義——

接著教我明白你在痛苦與死亡中的話語吧。

I have learnt the simple meaning of thy whispers in flowers and

sunshine--teach me to know thy words in pain and death.

270

遲來的夜之花朵，在早晨吻她時，

顫慄著，嘆息一聲，萎落在地上。

The night's flower was late when the morning kissed her,

she shivered and sighed and dropped to the ground.

從萬物的愁苦中，我聽見永恆之母的呻吟。

Through the sadness of all things

I hear the crooning of the Eternal Mother.

大地呀，我到你岸上時是陌生人，住在你屋內時是賓客，

出了你的門時則是朋友。

I came to your shore as a stranger, I lived in your house as a guest,

I leave your door as a friend, my earth.

當我離去時，讓我的思想到你那裡來，

如那夕陽的餘光，映在沉默的星天邊上。

Let my thoughts come to you, when I am gone,

like the afterglow of sunset at the margin of starry silence.

在我的心頭燃起那休憩的晚星吧，

然後讓黑夜向我微語著愛情。

Light in my heart the evening star of rest

and then let the night whisper to me of love.

我是一個在黑暗中的孩子。

我從夜的被單裡向您伸出雙手，母親。

I am a child in the dark.

I stretch my hands through the coverlet of night for thee, Mother.

白天的工作結束了。把我的臉掩藏在您的臂彎間吧，母親。

讓我入夢吧。

The day of work is done. Hide my face in your arms, Mother.

Let me dream.

277

集會時的燈光，亮了許久，會散時，燈便立刻滅了。

The lamp of meeting burns long;

it goes out in a moment at the parting.

278

當我死時，世界呀，請在你的沉默中，替我留下一句話：

「我曾愛過」。

One word keep for me in thy silence, O World, when I am dead,

"I have loved."

279

我們熱愛世界時便活在這世界上。

We live in this world when we love it.

280

讓亡者擁有不朽的名，但讓生者擁有不朽的愛。

Let the dead have the immortality of fame,

but the living the immortality of love.

281

我看見你，像那半醒的嬰孩在黎明微光中看見他的母親，

於是微笑著又睡去了。

I have seen thee as the half-awakened child sees his mother in

the dusk of the dawn and then smiles and sleeps again.

282

我將死而復死，以明白生之無窮。

I shall die again and again to know that life is inexhaustible.

283

當我和擁擠的人群一同在路上走過時，我看見您從陽臺上送
來的微笑，我高歌，忘卻了所有的喧嘩。

While I was passing with the crowd in the road I saw thy smile
from the balcony and I sang and forgot all noise.

284

愛就是充盈了的生命，正如盛滿了酒的酒杯。

Love is life in its fulness like the cup with its wine.

285

他們點了自己的燈，在他們的寺院內，吟唱自己的話語。
但是小鳥們卻在你的晨光中，唱著你的名字
——因為你的名字便是快樂。

They light their own lamps and sing their own words
in their temples.
But the birds sing thy name in thine own morning light,
--for thy name is joy.

286

領我到您靜寂的中心，讓我的心充滿歌聲。

Lead me in the centre of thy silence to fill my heart with songs.

287

那些自己選擇待在焰火嘶嘶的世界的，就讓他們活在那裡吧。

我的心卻渴望著您的繁星，我的上帝。

Let them live who choose in their own hissing world of fireworks.

My heart longs for thy stars, my God.

288

愛的痛苦繞著我的一生歌唱，就像洶湧的大海；而愛的快樂
卻像鳥兒們在花林裡歌唱。

Love's pain sang round my life like the unplumbed sea,

and love's joy sang like birds in its flowering groves.

289

假如您願意，就熄了燈吧。

我將明白您的黑暗，而且將喜愛它。

Put out the lamp when thou wishest.

I shall know thy darkness and shall love it.

290

當一日終了，我站在您面前時，您將看見我的疤，

知道我曾有許多傷口，但也有我醫治的方法。

When I stand before thee at the day's end thou shalt see my scars

and know that I had my wounds and also my healing.

291

總有一天，我要在另一個世界的晨光裡對你唱：

「我曾在大地的光裡，在眾人的愛裡，見過你了。」

Some day I shall sing to thee in the sunrise of some other world,

"I have seen thee before in the light of the earth,

in the love of man."

從其他日子裡飄浮到我生命裡的雲，不再落下雨點或
引起風暴了，只為我暮色的天空添加色彩。

Clouds come floating into my life from other days no longer to
shed rain or usher storm but to give colour to my sunset sky.

真理引起了反對它的狂風驟雨，那場風雨吹散了真理的種子。

Truth raises against itself the storm that scatters its seeds broadcast.

昨夜的風雨為今日的早晨冠以金色的和平。

The storm of the last night has crowned this morning
with golden peace.

295

真理仿佛帶了它的結論而來；而那結論卻產生了第二個結論。

Truth seems to come with its final word;

and the final word gives birth to its next.

296

他是有福的，因為他的名望並沒有比他的真實更光亮。

Blessed is he whose fame does not outshine his truth.

297

當我忘記自己的名字時，你甜蜜的名字充溢著我的心
——你便是早晨升起的太陽，驅散了雲霧。

Sweetness of thy name fills my heart when I forget mine

--like thy morning sun when the mist is melted.

298

靜悄悄的黑夜具有母親的美麗，

而吵鬧的白天具有孩子的美麗。

The silent night has the beauty of the mother

and the clamorous day of the child.

299

當人微笑時，世界愛著他；但他大笑時，世界卻怕了他。

The world loved man when he smiled.

The world became afraid of him when he laughed.

300

神等待人從智慧中重新獲得童年。

God waits for man to regain his childhood in wisdom.

讓我感到這個世界乃是你的愛所形成的吧，

那麼，我的愛也將幫助它。

Let me feel this world as thy love taking form,

then my love will help it.

你的陽光朝我心裡的冬日微笑，

從不懷疑它將在春日綻放花朵。

Thy sunshine smiles upon the winter days of my heart,

never doubting of its spring flowers.

神在祂的愛裡吻著「有涯」，人卻吻著「無涯」。

God kisses the finite in his love and man the infinite.

你越過不毛之年的沙漠，到達了圓滿的時刻。

Thou crossest desert lands of barren years

to reach the moment of fulfilment.

神的靜默使人的思想熟成為語言。

God's silence ripens man's thoughts into speech.

永恆的旅者呀，你可以在我的歌中找到你的足跡。

Thou wilt find, Eternal Traveller,

marks of thy footsteps across my songs.

讓我不至羞辱您吧，父親，您在您的孩子身上顯出您的光榮。

Let me not shame thee, Father,

who displayest thy glory in thy children.

這一天並不快樂。光在蹙額的雲下，像被責打的兒童，

灰白的臉上留著淚痕；風又呼號著，像世界受傷的哭聲。

但我知道，我正跋涉著去會我的朋友。

Cheerless is the day, the light under frowning clouds is like a

punished child with traces of tears on its pale cheeks,

and the cry of the wind is like the cry of a wounded world.

But I know I am travelling to meet my Friend.

309

今天晚上棕櫚葉在嚓嚓作響，海上有大浪，

滿月啊，就像世界在心脈悸跳。

從哪處不可知的天空，你在沉默裡帶來了愛的痛苦秘密？

To-night there is a stir among the palm leaves, a swell in the sea,

Full Moon, like the heart throb of the world.

From what unknown sky hast thou carried in thy silence the aching

secret of love?

310

我夢見一顆星，一座光明島嶼，我將在那裡出生。

在它轉瞬的閒暇深處，我的生命將成熟它的事業，

像陽光下的稻田。

I dream of a star, an island of light, where I shall be born

and in the depth of its quickening leisure my life will ripen its

works like the ricefield in the autumn sun.

311

雨中濕土的氣息，就像從渺小無聲的群眾那裡
傳來一陣巨大的讚美歌聲。

The smell of the wet earth in the rain rises like a great chant of
praise from the voiceless multitude of the insignificant.

312

愛會消失，我們卻無法將這個事實當作真理來接受。

That love can ever lose is a fact that we cannot accept as truth.

313

我們總有一天會明白，死亡永遠不能奪去靈魂曾獲得的一切。
因為靈魂所獲得的，和靈魂自身是一體的。

We shall know some day that death can never rob us of that which
our soul has gained, for her gains are one with herself.

神在我黃昏的微光中，帶著花到來。

這些往昔之花在祂的花籃中依舊鮮活。

God comes to me in the dusk of my evening with the flowers from

my past kept fresh in his basket.

主呀，當我生命的琴弦已能成調時，

祢的每一次撥弄，都能奏出愛的樂聲。

When all the strings of my life will be tuned, my Master,

then at every touch of thine will come out the music of love.

316

讓我真真實實地活著吧，我的上帝。

這樣，死對於我也就成了真實的了。

Let me live truly, my Lord, so that death to me become true.

人類的歷史正堅忍地等待著受辱者的勝利。

Man's history is waiting in patience for
the triumph of the insulted man.

這一刻，我感到你的目光正落在我心上，像那早晨陽光中的
沉默，落在已收穫的孤寂田野上。

I feel thy gaze upon my heart this moment like the sunny silence of
the morning upon the lonely field whose harvest is over.

在這喧嘩的、波濤起伏的海中，我渴望著歌詠之島。

I long for the Island of Songs across this heaving Sea of Shouts.

320

夜的序曲開始於夕陽西下的音樂，

開始於它對難以形容的黑暗所作的莊嚴讚歌。

The prelude of the night is commenced in the music of the sunset,

in its solemn hymn to the ineffable dark.

321

我攀上高峰，發現在名譽荒蕪不毛的高處，簡直找不到一個
遮身之地。我的引導者啊，引導我在光明逝去前，進入沉靜
的山谷裡吧。在那裡，一生的收穫將會成熟為黃金的智慧。

I have scaled the peak and found no shelter in fame's bleak and
barren height. Lead me, my Guide, before the light fades, into the
valley of quiet where life's harvest mellows into golden wisdom.

322

在黃昏的朦朧裡，好些東西看來都仿佛幻象一般——
尖塔的底層在黑暗裡消失了，樹頂像是墨水模糊的斑點。
我等待著黎明，而當我醒來的時候，
就會看到你在光明裡的城市。

Things look phantastic in this dimness of the dusk--the spires
whose bases are lost in the dark and tree tops like blots of ink.
I shall wait for the morning and wake up to see
thy city in the light.

323

在我的一生裡，也有貧乏和沉默的地域；
它們是我忙碌日子裡能得到日光與空氣的幾片空曠之地。

There are tracts in my life that are bare and silent. They are the
open spaces where my busy days had their light and air.

我未完的過去，從後邊纏繞在我身上，使我難以死去。
請釋放我吧。

Release me from my unfulfilled past clinging to me from behind
making death difficult.

「我相信你的愛。」讓這句話做我的最後的話。

Let this be my last word, that I trust in thy love.

最好的不會獨來，
它伴著一切同來.

The best does not come alone.
It comes with the company of the all.

新月集

家庭

我獨自在橫跨過田地的路上走著,夕陽像一個守財奴,正藏起它最後的金子。

白晝更加深沉地投入黑暗中,那已經收割的孤寂田地,默默躺在那裡。

天空裡突然響起一個男孩子尖銳的歌聲。他穿過看不見的黑暗,留下歌聲的轍痕跨過黃昏的靜謐。

他鄉村的家坐落在荒涼的邊上,在甘蔗田的後面,躲藏在香蕉樹、瘦長的檳榔樹、椰子樹和深綠色的賈克果樹陰影裡。

我在星光下孤寂的道路上停留了一會,我看見黑沉沉的大地鋪展在我面前,用她的手臂擁抱無數的家庭,那些家庭裡有著搖籃和床舖,有母親們的心和夜晚的燈,還有年輕的生命,他們滿心歡樂,卻渾然不知這樣的歡樂對於世界的價值。

THE HOME

I paced alone on the road across the field while the sunset was hiding
its last gold like a miser.

The daylight sank deeper and deeper into the darkness, and the
widowed land, whose harvest had been reaped, lay silent.

Suddenly a boy's shrill voice rose into the sky. He traversed the dark
unseen, leaving the track of his song across the hush of the evening.

His village home lay there at the end of the waste land, beyond the
sugar-cane field, hidden among the shadows of the banana and the
slender areca palm, the cocoa-nut and the dark green jack-fruit trees.

I stopped for a moment in my lonely way under the starlight, and saw
spread before me the darkened earth surrounding with her arms
countless homes furnished with cradles and beds, mothers' hearts and
evening lamps, and young lives glad with a gladness that knows
nothing of its value for the world.

海邊

孩子們匯集在這無邊世界的海邊。

無限的天穹靜止地臨於頭上，不息的海水在足下洶湧。孩子們匯集在這無邊世界的海邊，叫著跳著。

他們拿沙來建房屋，拿空貝殼來做遊戲。他們把落葉編成船，微笑地把它們放到廣大的深海上。孩子們在這世界的海邊，做他們的遊戲。

他們不知道怎樣泅水，他們不知道怎樣撒網。採珠的人為了珠下水，商人在他們的船上航行，小孩子們卻只把小圓石聚了又散。他們不蒐求藏寶；他們不知道怎樣撒網。

海水帶著笑掀起波浪，海邊也淡淡閃著笑意。致人死命的波濤，對孩子們唱著無意義的歌曲，像個搖動孩子搖籃的母親，海水和孩子們一同遊戲，海岸也淡淡閃著笑意。

孩子們匯集在這無邊的海邊。狂風暴雨飄遊在無跡的天空上，航船沉碎在無跡的海水裡，死亡正在外邊遊走，孩子們卻在遊戲。在這無邊世界的海邊上，孩子們匯集著。

ON THE SEASHORE

On the seashore of endless worlds children meet.

The infinite sky is motionless overhead and the restless water is boisterous. On the seashore of endless worlds the children meet with shouts and dances.

They build their houses with sand, and they play with empty shells. With withered leaves they weave their boats and smilingly float them on the vast deep. Children have their play on the seashore of worlds.

They know not how to swim, they know not how to cast nets. Pearl-fishers dive for pearls, merchants sail in their ships, while children gather pebbles and scatter them again. They seek not for hidden treasures, they know not how to cast nets.

The sea surges up with laughter, and pale gleams the smile of the sea-beach. Death-dealing waves sing meaningless ballads to the children, even like a mother while rocking her baby's cradle. The sea plays with children, and pale gleams the smile of the sea-beach.

On the seashore of endless worlds children meet. Tempest roams in the pathless sky, ships are wrecked in the trackless water, death is abroad and children play. On the seashore of endless worlds is the great meeting of children.

來源

流泛在孩子兩眼的睡眠，──有誰知道它是從什麼地方來
的？是的，有個謠傳，說它是住在螢火蟲朦朧照著林影裡的
仙村裡，在那個地方掛著兩個迷人又膽怯的蓓蕾。它便是從
那個地方來吻著孩子的雙眼。

當孩子睡時，微笑在他唇上浮動，──有誰知道他是從什麼
地方生出來的？是的，有個謠傳，說，一線新月的幼嫩清光，
觸著將消未消的秋雲邊上，微笑便從那個地方初生在一個浴
在清露裡的早晨夢中了。

甜蜜柔嫩的新鮮情景，在孩子的四肢上綻放，──有誰知道
他在什麼地方藏得這樣久？是的，當母親是一個少女的時候，
他已在愛的溫柔而沉靜的神祕中，潛伏在她的心裡。──甜
蜜柔嫩的新鮮情景，在孩子的四肢上綻放著。

THE SOURCE

The sleep that flits on baby's eyes--does anybody know from where it comes? Yes, there is a rumour that it has its dwelling where, in the fairy village among shadows of the forest dimly lit with glow-worms, there hang two shy buds of enchantment. From there it comes to kiss baby's eyes.

The smile that flickers on baby's lips when he sleep--does anybody know where it was born? Yes, there is a rumour that a young pale beam of a crescent moon touched the edge of a vanishing autumn cloud, and there the smile was first born in the dream of a dew-washed morning the smile that flickers on baby's lips when he sleeps.

The sweet, soft freshness that blooms on baby's limbs--does anybody know where it was hidden so long? Yes, when the mother was a young girl it lay pervading her heart in tender and silent mystery of love--the sweet, soft freshness that has bloomed on baby's limbs.

孩童之道

只要孩子願意，他此刻便可飛上天去。

他之所以不離開我們，並不是沒有緣故。

他愛把頭倚在媽媽的胸間，即使一刻不見她，也是不行的。

孩子知道各式各樣的聰明話，雖然世間的人很少懂得這些話的意義。

他之所以永不想說，並不是沒有緣故。

他要做的事，就是學習從媽媽嘴唇裡說出來的話。那就是他看來如此天真的緣故。

孩子有成堆的黃金與珠子，但他到這個世界上來，卻像一個乞丐。

他之所以這樣假裝了來，並不是沒有緣故。

這個可愛的、小小的、裸著身體的乞丐，之所以假裝著完全無助的樣子，是想要乞求母親愛的財富。

孩子在纖小的新月的世界裡，一切束縛都沒有。

他之所以放棄了他的自由，並不是沒有緣故。

他知道有無窮的快樂藏在媽媽心裡小小一隅，被媽媽親愛的手臂擁抱，其甜美遠勝過自由。

孩子永不知道如何哭泣。他所住的是完全的樂土。

他之所以要流淚，並不是沒有緣故。

BABY'S WAY

If baby only wanted to, he could fly up to heaven this moment.

It is not for nothing that he does not leave us.

He loves to rest his head on mother's bosom, and cannot ever bear to lose sight of her.

Baby knows all manner of wise words, though few on earth can understand their meaning.

It is not for nothing that he never wants to speak.

The one thing he wants is to learn mother's words from mother's lips.

That is why he looks so innocent.

Baby had a heap of gold and pearls, yet he came like a beggar onto this earth.

It is not for nothing he came in such a disguise.

This dear little naked mendicant pretends to be utterly helpless, so that he may beg for mother's wealth of love.

Baby was so free from every tie in the land of the tiny crescent moon.

It was not for nothing he gave up his freedom.

He knows that there is room for endless joy in mother's little corner of a heart, and it is sweeter far than liberty to be caught and pressed in her dear arms.

Baby never knew how to cry. He dwelt in the land of perfect bliss.

It is not for nothing he has chosen to shed tears.

雖然他用可愛臉蛋上的微笑，引逗得媽媽熱切的心向著他，然而他因為細故而發出的小小哭聲，卻編成了憐與愛的雙重牽絆。

Though with the smile of his dear face he draws mother's yearning heart to him, yet his little cries over tiny troubles weave the double bond of pity and love.

不被注意的花飾

啊，誰給那件小外衫染上顏色的，我的孩子，誰讓你溫軟的肢體穿上那件紅的小外衫？

你在早晨跑出來到天井裡玩，你，跑著就像搖搖欲跌似的。

但是誰給那件小外衫染上顏色的，我的孩子？

什麼事叫你大笑起來，我的小小的命芽兒？

媽媽站在門邊，微笑地望著你。

她拍著她的雙手，她的手鐲叮噹響著，你手裡拿著竹竿兒在跳舞，活像一個小小牧童。

但是什麼事叫你大笑起來的，我的小小的命芽兒？

喔，小乞丐，你雙手攀摟住媽媽的頭頸，要乞討些什麼？

喔，貪得無厭的心，要我把整個世界從天上摘下來，像摘一顆果子，把它放在你小小的玫瑰色的手掌上嗎？

喔，小乞丐，你要乞討些什麼？

風高興地帶走了你踝鈴的叮噹。

太陽微笑著，望著你的打扮。

當你睡在媽媽的臂彎裡，天空在上面望著你，而早晨躡手躡腳地走到你床前，吻著你的雙眼。

風高興地帶走了你踝鈴的叮噹。

仙鄉裡的夢婆飛過朦朧的天空，向你飛來。

THE UNHEEDED PAGEANT

Ah, who was it coloured that little frock, my child, and covered your sweet limbs with that little red tunic?

You have come out in the morning to play in the courtyard, tottering and tumbling as you run.

But who was it coloured that little frock, my child?

What is it makes you laugh, my little life-bud?

Mother smiles at you standing on the threshold.

She claps her hands and her bracelets jingle, and you dance with your bamboo stick in your hand like a tiny little shepherd.

But what is it makes you laugh, my little life-bud?

O beggar, what do you beg for, clinging to your mother's neck with both your hands?

O greedy heart, shall I pluck the world like a fruit from the sky to place it on your little rosy palm?

O beggar, what are you begging for?

The wind carries away in glee the tinkling of your anklet bells.

The sun smiles and watches your toilet. The sky watches over you when you sleep in your mother's arms, and the morning comes tiptoe to your bed and kisses your eyes.

The wind carries away in glee the tinkling of your anklet bells.

The fairy mistress of dreams is coming towards you, flying through the

在媽媽的心頭上，那世界之母，正和你坐在一塊兒。

那個向星星奏樂的人，正拿著他的橫笛，站在你的窗邊。

仙鄉裡的夢婆飛過朦朧的天空，向你飛來。

twilight sky.

The world-mother keeps her seat by you in your mother's heart.

He who plays his music to the stars is standing at your window with his flute.

And the fairy mistress of dreams is coming towards you, flying through the twilight sky.

盜眠者

誰從孩子的眼裡把睡眠偷了去呢？我一定要知道。

媽媽把她的水罐挾在腰間，走到近村汲水去了。

這是正午的時候，孩子們遊戲的時間已經過去了；池中的鴨子沉默無聲。

牧童躺在榕樹蔭下睡著了。

白鶴莊重而安靜地立在檬果樹邊的泥澤裡。

就在這個時候，盜眠者跑來從孩子的兩眼裡捉住睡眠，便飛去了。

當媽媽回來時，她看見孩子四肢著地地在屋裡爬著。

誰從孩子眼裡把睡眠偷去了？我一定要知道。我一定要找到她，把她鎖起來。

我一定要向那個黑洞裡張望，在這個洞裡，有一道小泉從圓的有皺紋的石上滴下來。

我一定要到醉花[1]林中沉寂的樹影裡搜尋，在這林中，鴿子在它們住的地方咕咕地叫，仙女的腳環在繁星滿天的靜夜裡叮噹地響。

我要在黃昏時，向靜靜的蕭蕭的竹林裡窺望，這林中，螢火

---

1 印度傳說，美女口中吐出香液，醉花始開。

SLEEP-STEALER

Who stole sleep from baby's eyes? I must know.

Clasping her pitcher to her waist mother went to fetch water from the village near by.

It was noon. The children's playtime was over; the ducks in the pond were silent.

The shepherd boy lay asleep under the shadow of the banyan tree.

The crane stood grave and still in the swamp near the mango grove.

In the meanwhile the Sleep-stealer came and, snatching sleep from baby's eyes, flew away.

When mother came back she found baby travelling the room over on all fours.

Who stole sleep from our baby's eyes? I must know. I must find her and chain her up.

I must look into that dark cave, where, through boulders and scowling stones, trickles a tiny stream.

I must search in the drowsy shade of the bakula grove, where pigeons coo in their corner, and fairies' anklets tinkle in the stillness of starry nights.

In the evening I will peep into the whispering silence of the bamboo forest, where fireflies squander their light, and will ask every creature I meet, "Can anybody tell me where the Sleep-stealer lives?"

蟲閃閃地耗費它們的光明，只要遇見一個人，我便要問他：

「誰能告訴我盜眠者住在什麼地方？」

誰從孩子的眼裡把睡眠偷了去呢？我一定要知道。

只要我能捉住她，怕不會給她一頓好教訓！

我要闖入她的巢穴，看她把所有偷來的睡眠藏在什麼地方。

我要把它都奪來，帶回家去。

我要把她的雙翼縛得緊緊的，把她放在河邊，然後叫她拿一根蘆葦在燈心草和睡蓮間釣魚為戲。

黃昏，街上已經收了市，村裡的孩子們都坐在媽媽的膝上時，夜鳥便會譏笑地在她耳邊說：

「你現在還想偷誰的睡眠呢？」

Who stole sleep from baby's eyes? I must know.

Shouldn't I give her a good lesson if I could only catch her!

I would raid her nest and see where she hoards all her stolen sleep.

I would plunder it all, and carry it home.

I would bind her two wings securely, set her on the bank of the river, and then let her play at fishing with a reed among the rushes and water-lilies.

When the marketing is over in the evening, and the village children sit in their mothers' laps, then the night birds will mockingly din her ears with:

"Whose sleep will you steal now?"

開始

「我是從哪兒來的，妳，是在哪兒把我撿起來的？」孩子問他的媽媽說。

她把孩子緊緊摟在胸前，半哭半笑地答道——

「你曾被我當作心願藏在心裡，我的寶貝。

「你曾存在於我孩童時玩的泥娃娃身上；每天早晨我用泥土塑造我的神像，那時我反覆塑了又捏碎了的就是你。

「你曾和我們的家庭守護神一同受到祀奉，我崇拜家神時也就崇拜了你。

「你曾活在我所有的希望和愛情裡，活在我的生命裡，我母親的生命裡。

「在主宰我們家庭的不死精靈膝上，你已經被撫育了好多代。

「當我做女孩子的時候，我的心花長開，你就像一股花香似地散發出來。

「你溫軟的柔情，在我青春的肢體上開了花，像太陽出來之前天空上的一片曙光。

「上天的第一寵兒，晨曦的孿生兄弟，你從世界的生命溪流浮泛而下，終於停泊在心頭。

「當我凝視你的臉蛋兒時，神祕之感淹沒了我；你這屬於一切的人，竟成了我的。

THE BEGINNING

"Where have I come from, where did you pick me up?" the baby asked
its mother.

She answered half crying, half laughing, and clasping the baby to her
breast,--"You were hidden in my heart as its desire, my darling.

You were in the dolls of my childhood's games; and when with clay I
made the image of my god every morning, I made and unmade you
then.

You were enshrined with our household deity, in his worship I
worshipped you.

In all my hopes and my loves, in my life, in the life of my mother you
have lived.

In the lap of the deathless Spirit who rules our home you have been
nursed for ages.

When in girlhood my heart was opening its petals, you hovered as a
fragrance about it.

Your tender softness bloomed in my youthful limbs, like a glow in the
sky before the sunrise.

Heaven's first darling, twin-born with the morning light, you have
floated down the stream of the world's life, and at last you have
stranded on my heart.

As I gaze on your face, mystery overwhelms me; you who belong to all

「為了怕失掉你，我把你緊緊摟在胸前。是什麼魔術把這世界的寶貝引到我這雙纖小的手臂裡來呢？」

have become mine.

For fear of losing you I hold you tight to my breast. What magic has snared the world's treasure in these slender arms of mine?"

孩子的世界

我願能在我孩子的世界中心，占一角清淨地。

我知道有星星同他說話，天空也在他面前垂下，用它傻傻的雲朵和彩虹來愉悅他。

那些大家以為是啞了的人，那些看上去像是永不會走動的人，都帶來他們的故事，捧著滿裝五顏六色玩具的盤子，匍匐來到他的窗前。

我願我能在橫過孩子心中的道路上遊行，解脫了一切的束縛；在那裡，使者奉了無所謂的使命奔走於無歷史的諸王之國間；在那裡，理智以她的法律造為紙鳶而飛放，真理也使事實從桎梏中自由。

BABY'S WORLD

I wish I could take a quiet corner in the heart of my baby's very own world.

I know it has stars that talk to him, and a sky that stoops down to his face to amuse him with its silly clouds and rainbows.

Those who make believe to be dumb, and look as if they never could move, come creeping to his window with their stories and with trays crowded with bright toys.

I wish I could travel by the road that crosses baby's mind, and out beyond all bounds;

Where messengers run errands for no cause between the kingdoms of kings of no history;

Where Reason makes kites of her laws and flies them, and Truth sets Fact free from its fetters.

時候與原因

當我給你五顏六色玩具的時候，我的孩子，我明白了為什麼雲上水上是這樣的色彩繽紛，為什麼花朵染上絢爛的顏色——就在我給你五顏六色玩具的時候，我的孩子。

當我唱著歌使你跳舞的時候，我真的知道了為什麼樹葉響著樂聲，為什麼波浪把它們合唱的聲音送進靜聽著的大地心頭——就在我唱著歌使你跳舞的時候。

當我把糖果送到你貪得無厭雙手上的時候，我知道了為什麼花萼裡會有蜜，為什麼水果裡會祕密地充溢了甜汁——就在我把糖果送到你貪得無厭雙手上的時候。

當我吻著你的臉蛋兒叫你微笑的時候，我的寶貝，我的確明白了晨光裡從天上流洩的是什麼樣的快樂，而夏天的微風吹拂在我身上的又是什麼樣的爽快——就在我吻著你的臉蛋兒叫你微笑的時候。

WHEN AND WHY

When I bring you coloured toys, my child, I understand why there is
such a play of colours on clouds, on water, and why flowers are painted
in tints--when I give coloured toys to you, my child.

When I sing to make you dance, I truly know why there is music in
leaves, and why waves send their chorus of voices to the heart of the
listening earth--when I sing to make you dance.

When I bring sweet things to your greedy hands, I know why there is
honey in the cup of the flower, and why fruits are secretly filled with
sweet juice--when I bring sweet things to your greedy hands.

When I kiss your face to make you smile, my darling, I surely
understand what pleasure streams from the sky in morning light, and
what delight the summer breeze brings to my body--when I kiss you to
make you smile.

責備

為什麼你眼裡有眼淚，我的孩子？

他們真可怕，常常無謂地責備你！

你寫字時墨水汙了你的手和臉——這就是他們罵你骯髒的緣故嗎？

呀，呸！他們也敢因為圓圓的月兒用墨水塗了臉，便罵它骯髒嗎？

他們總要為了每一件小事去責備你，我的孩子。他們總是無謂地尋人錯處。

你遊戲時扯破了衣服——這就是他們說你不整潔的緣故嗎？

呀，呸！秋之晨從它破碎的雲衣中露出微笑。那麼，他們要叫它什麼呢？

他們對你說什麼話，儘管不去理睬，我的孩子。

他們把你做錯的事長長地記了一筆帳。

誰都知道你是十分喜歡糖果的——這就是他們稱你做貪婪的緣故嗎？

呀，呸！我們是喜歡你的，那麼，他們要叫我們什麼呢？

DEFAMATION

Why are those tears in your eyes, my child?

How horrid of them to be always scolding you for nothing?

You have stained your fingers and face with ink while writing—is that why they call you dirty?

O, fie! Would they dare to call the full moon dirty because it has smudged its face with ink?

For every little trifle they blame you, my child. They are ready to find fault for nothing.

You tore your clothes while playing--is that why they call you untidy?

O, fie! What would they call an autumn morning that smiles through its ragged clouds?

Take no heed of what they say to you, my child.

Take no heed of what they say to you, my child.

They make a long list of your misdeeds. Everybody knows how you love sweet things--is that why they call you greedy?

O, fie! What then would they call us who love you?

審判官

你想說他什麼儘管說吧，但是我知道我孩子的短處。

我愛他並不因為他好，只是因為他是我小小的孩子。

你如果把他的好處與壞處兩兩相權，恐怕你就會知道他是如何的可愛吧？

當我必須責罰他的時候，他更成為我生命的一部分了。

當我使他流出眼淚時，我的心也和他一同哭了。

只有我才有權去罵他，去責罰他，因為只有熱愛人的才可以懲戒人。

THE JUDGE

Say of him what you please, but I know my child's failings.

I do not love him because he is good, but because he is my little child.

How should you know how dear he can be when you try to weigh his merits against his faults?

When I must punish him he becomes all the more a part of my being.

When I cause his tears to come my heart weeps with him.

I alone have a right to blame and punish, for he only may chastise who loves.

玩具

孩子，你真是快活呀，整個早晨都坐在泥土裡，耍著折下來的小樹枝兒。

我微笑地看你在那裡耍著那根折下來的小樹枝兒。

我正忙著算帳，一小時一小時在那裡加疊數字。

也許你在看我，想道：這種好沒趣的遊戲，竟把你一早晨的好時光都浪費掉了！

孩子，我忘了聚精會神玩耍樹枝與泥餅的方法了。

我尋求貴重的玩具，收集金塊與銀塊。

你呢，無論找到什麼便去做你快樂的遊戲，我呢，卻把我的時間與力氣都浪費在那些我永不能得到的東西上。

我在我脆薄的獨木船裡掙紮著要航過欲望之海，竟忘了我也是在那裡遊戲的了。

PLAYTHINGS

Child, how happy you are sitting in the dust, playing with a broken twig all the morning.

I smile at your play with that little bit of a broken twig.

I am busy with my accounts, adding up figures by the hour.

Perhaps you glance at me and think, "What a stupid game to spoil your morning with!"

Child, I have forgotten the art of being absorbed in sticks and mud-pies.

I seek out costly playthings, and gather lumps of gold and silver.

With whatever you find you create your glad games, I spend both my time and my strength over things I never can obtain.

In my frail canoe I struggle to cross the sea of desire, and forget that I too am playing a game.

天文家

我不過說：「當傍晚圓圓的滿月掛在迦曇波[2]的枝頭時，有人能去捉住它嗎？」

哥哥卻對我笑道：「孩子呀，你真是我見過最最傻氣的孩子。月亮離我們這樣遠，誰能去捉住它呢？」

我說：「哥哥，你真傻！當媽媽向窗外探望，微笑著往下看我們遊戲時，你也能說她遠嗎？」

哥哥還是說：「你這個傻孩子！但是，孩子，你到哪裡去找一個大得能逮住月亮的網呢？」

我說：「你自然可以用雙手去捉住它呀。」

但是哥哥還是笑著說：「你真是我見過最最傻氣的孩子！如果月亮走近了，你便知道它有多麼大了。」

我說：「哥哥，你們學校裡所教的，真是沒有用呀！當媽媽低下臉兒跟我們親嘴時，她的臉看來也是很大的嗎？」

但哥哥還是說：「你真是一個傻孩子。」

---

2 迦曇波，原名 kadam，亦作 kadamba，學名 namleacadamba，意譯「白花」，即曇花。

THE ASTRONOMER

I only said, "When in the evening the round full moon gets entangled among the branches of that Kadam tree, couldn't somebody catch it?"

But dâdâ laughed at me and said, "Baby,

you are the silliest child I have ever known. The moon is ever so far from us, how could anybody catch it?"

I said, "Dâdâ how foolish you are! When mother looks out of her window and smiles down at us playing, would you call her faraway?"

Still said, "You are a stupid child! But, baby, where could you find a net big enough to catch the moon with?"

I said, "Surely you could catch it with your hands."

But dâdâ laughed and said, "You are the silliest child I have known. If it came nearer, you would see how big the moon is."

I said, "Dâdâ, what nonsense they teach at your school! When mother bends her face down to kiss us does her face look very big?"

But still dâdâ says, "You are a stupid child."

雲與波

媽媽，住在雲端的人對我喚道——

「我們從醒來時便遊戲到白日終止。

我們與黃金色的曙光遊戲，我們與銀白色的月亮遊戲。」

我問道：「但是，我要怎麼到你那裡去呢？」

他們答道：「你到地球的邊上來，舉手向天，就可以被接到雲端裡來了。」

「我媽媽在家裡等我呢，」我說，「我怎麼能離她而來呢？」

於是他們微笑著浮游而去。

但是我知道一件比這個更好的遊戲，媽媽。

我做雲，你做月亮。

我用兩隻手遮蓋你，我們的屋頂就是青碧的天空。

住在波浪上的人對我喚道——

「我們從早晨歌唱到晚上；我們前進又前進地旅行，也不知我們所經過的是什麼地方。」

我問道：「但是，我要怎麼加入你們的隊伍呢？」

他們告訴我說：「來到岸旁，站在那裡，緊閉你的兩眼，你就被帶到波浪上來了。」

我說：「傍晚的時候，我媽媽常要我在家裡——我怎麼能離她而去呢！」

CLOUDS AND WAVES

Mother, the folk who live up in the clouds call out to me--

"We play from the time we wake till the day ends.

We play with the golden dawn, we play with the silver moon.

I ask, "But, how am I to get up to you?" They answer, "Come to the edge of the earth, lift up your hands to the sky, and you will be taken up into the clouds."

"My mother is waiting for me at home," I say. "How can I leave her and come?"

Then they smile and float away.

But I know a nicer game than that, mother.

I shall be the cloud and you the moon.

I shall cover you with both my hands, and our house-top will be the blue sky.

The folk who live in the waves call out to me--

"We sing from morning till night; on and on we travel and know not where we pass."

I ask, "But, how am I to join you?" They tell me, "Come to the edge of the shore and stand with your eyes tight shut, and you will be carried out upon the waves."

I say, "My mother always wants me at home in the evening--how can I leave her and go?"

於是他們微笑著，跳舞著奔流過去。

但是我知道一件比這個更好的遊戲。

我是波浪，你是陌生的岸。

我奔流而進，前進，前進，笑哈哈地撞碎在你的膝上。

世界上就沒有一個人會知道我倆在什麼地方。

Then they smile, dance and pass by.

But I know a better game than that.

I will be the waves and you will be a strange shore.

I shall roll on and on and on, and break upon your lap with laughter.

And no one in the world will know where we both are.

金色花

假如我變了一朵金色花[3]，只是為了好玩，長在那棵樹的高枝上，笑哈哈地在風中搖擺，又在新生的樹葉上跳舞，媽媽，妳會認識我嗎？

妳要是叫道：「孩子，你在哪裡呀？」我便暗暗地在那裡竊笑，卻一聲兒不響。

我要悄悄地開放花瓣兒，看著妳工作。

當妳沐浴後，濕髮披在兩肩，穿過金色花的林蔭，走到妳做禱告的小庭院時，妳會嗅到這花的香氣，卻不知道這香氣是從我身上來的。

當你吃過中飯，坐在窗前讀《羅摩衍那》[4]，那棵樹的陰影落在妳的頭髮與膝上時，我便要投下我小小的影子在妳的書頁上，投在妳所讀的地方。

但是妳猜得出這就是妳孩子的小影子嗎？

---

3 金色花，原名 champa，亦作 champak，學名 michcliachampaca，印度聖樹，木蘭花屬植物，開金黃色碎花。譯名亦作「瞻波伽」或「占博伽」。

4 《羅摩衍那》（ramayana）為印度敘事詩，相傳系蟻垤（valmiki）所作。今傳本形式約為西元二世紀間所形成。全書分為七卷，共二萬四千頌，皆系敘述羅摩生平之作。羅摩即羅摩犍陀羅。十車王之子，悉多之夫。他於第二世（tretayaga）入世，為毗濕奴神第七化身。印人看他為英雄，有崇拜他如神的。

THE CHAMPA FLOWER

Supposing I became a champa flower, just for fun, and grew on a branch high up that tree, and shook in the wind with laughter and danced upon the newly budded leaves, would you know me, mother?

You would call, "Baby, where are you?" and I should laugh to myself and keep quite quiet.

I should slyly open my petals and watch you at your work.

When after your bath, with wet hair spread on your shoulders, you walked through the shadow of the champa tree to the little court where you say your prayers, you would notice the scent of the flower, but not know that it came from me.

When after the midday meal you sat at the window reading Ramayana, and the tree's shadow fell over your hair and your lap, I should fling my wee little shadow on to the page of your book, just where you were reading.

But would you guess that it was the tiny shadow of your little child?

當妳黃昏時拿了燈到牛棚裡去，我便要突然再落到地上來，
又成了妳的孩子，求妳講個故事給我聽。

「你到哪裡去了，你這壞孩子？」

「我不告訴妳，媽媽。」這就是妳和我會說的話。

When in the evening you went to the cow-shed with the lighted lamp in your hand, I should suddenly drop on to the earth again and be your own baby once more, and beg you to tell me a story.

"Where have you been, you naughty child?"

"I won't tell you, mother." That's what you and I would say then.

仙人世界

如果人們知道我的國王的宮殿在哪，它就會消失在空氣中。

牆壁是白色的銀，屋頂是耀眼的金。

皇后住在有七個庭院的宮苑裡；她戴的一串珠寶，值得整整七個王國的全部財富。

不過，讓我悄悄告訴妳，媽媽，我的國王的宮殿究竟在哪裡。

它就在我們陽台的角上，在那栽著杜爾茜花的花盆處。

公主躺在遠遠隔著七重不可逾越之海的那一岸沉睡著。

除了我自己，世界上便沒有人能夠找到她。

她臂上有鐲子，她耳上掛著珍珠；她的頭髮拖到地板上。

當我用魔杖輕觸她時，她就會醒來，當她微笑時，珠玉將會從她唇邊落下。

不過，讓我在妳的耳邊悄悄告訴妳，媽媽；她就住在我們陽台的角上，在那栽著杜爾茜花的花盆處。

當妳要到河裡洗澡時，便走上屋頂的那座陽台來吧。

我就坐在牆的陰影所會聚的一個角落裡。

我只讓小貓兒跟我在一起，因為它知道那故事裡的理髮匠住的地方。

FAIRYLAND

If people came to know where my king's palace is, it would vanish into
the air.

The walls are of white silver and the roof of shining gold.

The queen lives in a palace with seven courtyards, and she wears
a jewel that cost all the wealth of seven kingdoms.

But let me tell you, mother, in a whisper, where my king's palace is.

It is at the corner of our terrace where the pot of the tulsi plant stands.

The princess lies sleeping on the far-away shore of the seven impassable
seas.

There is none in the world who can find her but myself.

She has bracelets on her arms and pearl drops in her ears; her hair
sweeps down upon the floor.

She will wake when I touch her with my magic wand, and jewels will
fall from her lips when she smiles.

But let me whisper in your ear, mother; she is there in the corner of
our terrace where the pot of the tulsi plant
stands.

When it is time for you to go to the river for your bath, step up to that
terrace on the roof.

不過，讓我在妳耳邊悄悄告訴妳，那故事裡的理髮匠到底住在哪裡。

他住的地方，就在陽台的角上，在那栽著杜爾茜花的花盆處。

I sit in the corner where the shadows of the walls meet together.

Only puss is allowed to come with me, for she knows where the barber in the story lives.

But let me whisper, mother, in your ear where the barber in the story lives.

It is at the corner of the terrace where the pot of the tulsi plant stands.

流放之地

媽媽，天空上的光成了灰色的；我不知道是什麼時候了。

我玩得怪沒勁兒的，所以到妳這裡來了。是星期六，是我們的休息日。

放下妳的活計，媽媽；坐在靠窗的一邊，告訴我童話裡特潘塔沙漠在什麼地方？

雨的影子遮掩了整個白天。

兇猛的電光用它的爪子撓著天空。

當烏雲轟轟作響，當漫天雷鳴，我總愛心裡帶著恐懼爬伏到妳的身上。

當大雨傾瀉在竹葉子上好幾個鐘頭，而我們的窗戶為狂風震得格格作響時，我就愛獨自和妳坐在屋裡，媽媽，聽妳講童話裡特潘塔沙漠的故事。

它在哪裡，媽媽，在哪一個海洋的岸上，在哪些個山峰的腳下，在哪一個國王的國土裡？

田地上沒有此疆彼壤的界石，也沒有村人在黃昏時走回家，或婦人在樹林裡撿拾枯枝而捆載到市場上去的道路。沙地上只有一小塊一小塊的黃色草地，只有一株樹，那對聰明的老鳥兒在那裡做窩，那個地方就是特潘塔沙漠。

我能夠想像得到，就在這樣一個烏雲密佈的日子，國王的年

THE LAND OF THE EXILE

Mother, the light has grown grey in the sky; I do not know what the time is.

There is no fun in my play, so I have come to you. It is Saturday, our holiday.

Leave off your work, mother; sit here by the window and tell me where the desert of Tepântar in the fairy tale is?

The shadow of the rains has covered the day from end to end.

The fierce lightning is scratching the sky with its nails.

When the clouds rumble and it thunders, I love to be afraid in my heart and cling to you.

When the heavy rain patters for hours on the bamboo leaves, and our windows shake and rattle at the gusts of wind, I like to sit alone in the room, mother, with you, and hear you talk about the desert of Tepântar in the fairy tale.

Where is it, mother, on the shore of what sea, at the foot of what hills, in the kingdom of what king?

There are no hedges there to mark the fields, no footpath across it by which the villagers reach their village in the evening, or the woman who gathers dry sticks in the forest can bring her load to the market.

With patches of yellow grass in the sand and only one tree where the pair of wise old birds have their nest, lies the desert of Tepântar.

輕兒子，如何獨自騎著一匹灰馬，走過這個沙漠，去尋找那被囚在未知重洋外巨人宮殿裡的公主。

當雨霧在遙遠的天空降下，當電光像一陣突發的痛楚痙攣似地閃射，他可記得他不幸的母親，為國王所棄，正清掃牛棚，眼裡流淚，就在他騎馬走過童話裡特潘塔沙漠的時候？

看，媽媽，一天還沒有完，天色就差不多黑了，那邊村莊的路上沒有什麼旅客了。

牧童早就從牧場上回家，人們都已從田地裡回來，坐在他們草屋簷下的草席上，眼望著陰沉的雲塊。

媽媽，我把我所有的書本都放在書架上了——不要叫我現在做功課。

當我長大了，大得像爸爸一樣的時候，我將會學到必須學的東西。

但是，今天妳可得告訴我，媽媽，童話裡特潘塔沙漠在什麼地方？

I can imagine how, on just such a cloudy day, the young son of the king is riding alone on a grey horse through the desert, ins each of the princess who lies imprisoned in the giant's palace across that unknown water.

When the haze of the rain comes down in the distant sky, and lightning starts up like a sudden fit of pain, does he remember his unhappy mother, abandoned by the king, sweeping the cow-stall and wiping her eyes, while he rides through the desert of Tepântar in the fairy tale?

See, mother, it is almost dark before the day is over, and there are no travelers yonder on the village road.

The shepherd boy has gone home early from the pasture, and men have left their fields to sit on mats under the eaves of their huts, watching the scowling clouds.

Mother, I have left all my books on the shelf--do not ask me to do my lessons now.

When I grow up and am big like my father, I shall learn all that must be learnt.

But just for to-day, tell me, mother, where the desert of Tepântar in the fairy tale is?

雨天

烏雲很快聚攏在森林黝黑的邊緣上。

孩子，不要出去呀！

湖邊的一行棕樹，向暝暗的天空撞著頭；羽毛零亂的烏鴉，

靜悄悄棲在羅望子的枝上，河的東岸正被烏沉沉的暝色侵襲。

我們的牛繫在籬上，高聲鳴叫。

孩子，在這裡等著，等我先把牛牽進牛棚裡去。

許多人都擠在池水泛溢的田間，捉那從溢滿的池中逃出來的

魚兒，雨水成了小河，流過狹街，像一個嬉笑的孩子從他媽

媽那裡跑開，故意要惱她一樣。

聽呀，有人在淺灘上喊船夫呢。

孩子，天色暝暗了，渡頭的擺渡船已經停了。

天空好像是在滂沱的雨上快跑著；河裡的水喧叫而且暴躁；

婦人們早已拿著汲滿水的水罐，從恆河畔匆匆地回家了。

夜裡用的燈，一定要預備好。

孩子，不要出去呀！

到市場去的大道已沒人走，到河邊去的小路又很溼滑。風在

竹林裡咆哮著，掙扎著，像一隻落在網中的獸。

THE RAINY DAY

Sullen clouds are gathering fast over the black fringe of the forest.

O child, do not go out!

The palm trees in a row by the lake are smiting their heads against the dismal sky; the crows with their draggled wings are silent on the tamarind branches, and the eastern bank of the river is haunted by a deepening gloom.

Our cow is lowing loud, tied at the fence.

O child, wait here till I bring her into the stall.

Men have crowded into the flooded field to catch the fishes as they escape from the overflowing ponds; the rain water is running in rills through the narrow lanes like a laughing boy who has run away from his mother to tease her.

Listen, someone is shouting for the boatman at the ford.

O child, the daylight is dim, and the crossing at the ferry is closed.

The sky seems to ride fast upon the madly-rushing rain; the water in the river is loud and impatient; women have hastened home early from the Ganges with their filled pitchers.

The evening lamps must be made ready.

O child, do not go out!

The road to the market is desolate, the lane to the river is slippery. The wind is roaring and struggling among the bamboo branches like a wild beast tangled in a net.

紙船

我每天把紙船一艘艘放在急流的溪中。

我在紙船上用大黑字體寫下我的名字和我住的村名。

我希望住在異地的人會得到這艘紙船,知道我是誰。

我把園中的秀利花載在我的小船上,希望這些黎明開的花能在夜裡被平平安安地帶到岸上。

我將紙船擲到水裡,仰望天空,看見小朵的雲正張著滿鼓著風的白帆。

我不知道天上有我的什麼遊伴把這些船放下來同我的船比賽!夜來了,我的臉埋在手臂裡,夢見我的紙船在子夜的星光下緩緩地浮泛前去。

睡仙坐在船裡,帶著裝滿了夢的籃子。

PAPER BOATS

Day by day I float my paper boats one by one down the running stream.

In big black letters I write my name on them and the name of the village where I live.

I hope that someone in some strange land will find them and know who I am.

I load my little boats with shiuli flowers from our garden, and hope that these blooms of the dawn will be carried safely to land in the night.

I launch my paper boats and look up into the sky and see the little clouds setting their white bulging sails.

I know not what playmate of mine in the sky sends them down the air to race with my boats!

When night comes I bury my face in my arms and dream that my paper boats float on and on under the midnight stars.

The fairies of sleep are sailing in them, and the lading is their baskets full of dreams.

水手

船夫曼特胡的船隻停泊在拉琪根琪碼頭。

這艘船無用地裝載著黃麻，無所事事停泊在那裡已經好久了。

只要他肯把船借給我，我就給它安裝一百支槳，揚起五個或六個或七個布帆來。

我絕不把它駕駛到愚蠢的市場上去。

我將航遍仙人世界裡的七大洋和十三河道。

但是，媽媽，妳不要躲在角落裡為我哭泣。

我不會像羅摩犍陀羅那樣，到森林中去，一去十四年才回來。

我將成為故事中的王子，把我的船裝滿我所喜歡的東西。

我將帶我的朋友阿細和我作伴，我們要快快樂樂地航行於仙人世界裡的七大洋和十三河道。

我將在絕早的晨光裡張帆航行。

中午，妳正在池塘裡洗澡的時候，我們便在一個陌生國王的國土上了。

我們將經過特浦尼淺灘，把特潘塔沙漠拋落在我們的後邊。

當我們回來的時候，天色快黑了，我將告訴妳我們所見的一切。

我將越過仙人世界裡的七大洋和十三河道。

THE SAILOR

The boat of the boatman Madhu is moored at the wharf of Rajgunj.

It is uselessly laden with jute, and has been lying there idle for ever so long.

If he would only lend me his boat, I should man her with a hundred oars, and hoist sails, five or six or seven.

I should never steer her to stupid markets. I should sail the seven seas and the thirteen rivers of fairyland.

But, mother, you won't weep for me in a corner.

I am not going into the forest like Ramachandra to come back only after fourteen years.

I shall become the prince of the story, and fill my boat with whatever I like.

I shall take my friend Ashu with me. We shall sail merrily across the seven seas and the thirteen rivers of fairyland.

We shall set sail in the early morning light.

When at noontide you are bathing at the pond, we shall be in the land of a strange king.

We shall pass the ford of Tirpurni, and leave behind us the desert of Tepântar.

When we come back it will be getting dark, and I shall tell you of all that we have seen.

I shall cross the seven seas and the thirteen rivers off airy land.

對岸

我想到河的對岸去。

在那邊，好些船隻一行繫在竹竿上；

人們在早晨乘船渡到那邊去，肩上扛著犁頭，去耕耘他們遠處的田；

在那兒，牧人使他們鳴叫著的牛游到河旁的牧場去；

黃昏時，他們都回家了，只留下豺狼在這長滿野草的島上哀叫。

媽媽，如果妳不在意，我長大的時候，要做這渡船的船夫。

據說有好些古怪的池塘藏在這個高岸之後。

雨過去了，一群一群野鶩飛到那裡，茂盛的蘆葦在岸邊生長，水鳥在那裡下蛋；

竹雞帶著舞動的尾巴，將它們細小的足印印在潔淨的軟泥上；

黃昏時，長草頂著白花，邀月光在長草的波浪上浮游。

媽媽，如果妳不在意，我長大的時候，要做這渡船的船夫。

我要自此岸至彼岸，渡過來，渡過去，所有村中正在那兒沐浴的男孩女孩，都要詫異地望著我。

太陽升到中天，早晨變為正午了，我將跑到妳那裡去，說道：

「媽媽，我餓了！」

一天完了，影子伏在樹底下，我便要在黃昏中回家來。

194

THE FURTHER BANK

I long to go over there to the further bank of the river,

Where those boats are tied to the bamboo poles in a line;

Where men cross over in their boats in the morning with plough son
their shoulders to till their far-away fields;

Where the cowherds make their lowing cattle swim across to the
riverside pasture;

Whence they all come back home in the evening, leaving the jackals to
howl in the island overgrown with weeds,

Mother, if you don't mind, I should like to become the boatman of the
ferry when I am grown up.

They say there are strange pools hidden behind that high bank,

Where flocks of wild ducks come when the rains are over, and thick
reeds grow round the margins where water birds lay their eggs;

Where snipes with their dancing tails stamp their tiny footprints upon
the clean soft mud;

Where in the evening the tall grasses crested with white flowers invite
the moonbeam to float upon their waves.

Mother, if you don't mind, I should like to become the boatman of the
ferryboat when I am grown up.

I shall cross and cross back from bank to bank, and all the boys and
girls of the village will wonder at me while they are bathing.

我將永不同爸爸那樣，離開妳到城裡作事。

媽媽，如果妳不在意，我長大的時候，要做這渡船的船夫。

When the sun climbs the mid sky and morning wears on to noon, is hall come running to you, saying, "Mother, I am hungry!"

When the day is done and the shadows cower under the trees, is hall come back in the dusk.

I shall never go away from you into the town to work like father.

Mother, if you don't mind, I should like to become the boatman of the ferryboat when I am grown up.

花的學校

當雷雲在天上轟響，六月陣雨落下時，

潤濕的東風走過荒野，在竹林中吹著口笛。

於是一群一群花從無人知曉的地方突然跑出來，在綠草上狂
歡跳舞。

媽媽，我真的覺得那群花朵在地下的學校裡上學。

它們關了門做功課，如果它想在放學以前出來遊戲，它們的
老師會罰它們靠牆站。

雨一來，它們便放假了。

樹枝在林中互相碰觸，綠葉在狂風裡蕭蕭地響，雷雲拍著大
手，花孩子們便在那時穿了紫的、黃的、白的衣裳衝出來。

妳可知道，媽媽，它們的家是在天上，在星星所住的地方。

妳沒有看見它們如何急著要到那兒去嗎？妳不知道它們為什
麼那樣急急忙忙嗎？

我自然能猜得出它們是對誰揚起雙臂來：它們也有它們的媽
媽，就像我有我自己的媽媽一樣。

THE FLOWER-SCHOOL

When storm clouds rumble in the sky and June showers come down,
The moist east wind comes marching over the heath to blow its
bagpipes among the bamboos.

Then crowds of flowers come out of a sudden, from nobody knows
where, and dance upon the grass in wild glee.

Mother, I really think the flowers go to school underground.

They do their lessons with doors shut, and if they want to come out to
play before it is time, their master makes them stand in a corner.

When the rains come they have their holidays.

Branches clash together in the forest, and the leaves rustle in the wild
wind, the thunder-clouds clap their giant hands and the flower
children rush out in dresses of pink and yellow and white.

Do you know, mother, their home is in the sky, where the stars are.

Haven't you seen how eager they are to get there? Don't you know
why they are in such a hurry?

Of course, I can guess to whom they raise their arms: they have their
mother as I have my own.

商人

媽媽，讓我們想像，妳待在家裡，我到異邦去旅行。

再想像，我的船已經裝得滿滿地在碼頭上等候下錨了。

現在，媽媽，好生想一想再告訴我，回來的時候我要帶些什麼給妳。

媽媽，你要一壘一壘的黃金嗎？

在金河的兩岸，田野裡全是金色的稻實。

在林蔭的路上，金色花也一朵朵落在地上。

我要為妳把它們全都收拾起來，放在好幾百個籃子裡。

媽媽，妳要秋天雨點般大的珍珠嗎？

我要渡海到珍珠島的岸上去。

那個地方，在清晨的曙光裡，珠子在草地的野花上顫動，珠子落在綠草上，珠子被洶狂的海浪一大把一大把撒在沙灘上。

我的哥哥呢，我要送他一對有翼的馬，能在雲端上飛翔。

爸爸呢，我要帶一支有魔力的筆給他，他還沒有感覺，筆就寫出字來了。

妳呢，媽媽，我定要把那值七個王國的首飾箱和珠寶送給妳。

THE MERCHANT

Imagine, mother, that you are to stay at home and I am to travel into
strange lands.

Imagine that my boat is ready at the landing fully laden.

Now think well, mother, before you say what I shall bring for you
when I come back.

Mother, do you want heaps and heaps of gold?

There, by the banks of golden streams, fields are full of golden harvest.

And in the shade of the forest path the golden champa flowers drop
on the ground.

I will gather them all for you in many hundred baskets.

Mother, do you want pearls big as the raindrops of autumn?

I shall cross to the pearl island shore. There in the early morning light
pearls tremble on the meadow flowers, pearls drop on the grass, and
pearls are scattered on the sand in spray by the wild sea-waves.

My brother shall have a pair of horses with wings to fly among the
clouds.

For father I shall bring a magic pen that, without his knowing, will
write of itself.

For you, mother, I must have the casket and jewel that cost seven kings
their kingdoms.

同情

如果我只是一隻小狗，而不是妳的孩子，親愛的媽媽，當我想吃妳盤裡的東西時，妳要向我說「不」嗎？

妳要趕開我，對我說道：「滾開，你這淘氣的小狗」嗎？

那麼，走吧，媽媽，走吧！當妳叫喚我的時候，我就永不到妳那裡去，也永不要妳再餵我吃東西。

如果我只是一隻綠色的小鸚鵡，而不是妳孩子，親愛的媽媽，妳要把我緊緊鎖住，怕我飛走嗎？

妳要對我搖妳的手，說：「這是多麼不知感恩的賤鳥呀！整夜盡在咬牠的鏈子」嗎？

那麼，走吧，媽媽，走吧！我要跑到樹林裡去；我永不再讓妳抱我在妳的臂彎裡。

SYMPATHY

If I were only a little puppy, not your baby, mother dear, would
you say "No" to me if I tried to eat from your dish?

Would you drive me off, saying to me, "Get away, you naughty little
puppy?"

Then go, mother, go! I will never come to you when you call me, and
never let you feed me anymore.

If I were only a little green parrot, and not your baby, mother dear,
would you keep me chained lest I should fly away?

Would you shake your finger at me and say, "What an ungrateful
wretch of a bird! It is gnawing at its chain day and night?"

Then, go, mother, go! I will run away into the woods; I will
never let you take me in your arms again.

職業

早晨，鐘敲十下的時候，我沿著我們的小巷到學校去。

每天我都遇見那個小販，他叫道：「鐲子呀，亮晶晶的鐲子！」

他沒有什麼事急著要做，他沒有哪條街一定要走，他沒有什麼地方一定要去，他沒有什麼時間一定要回家。

我願意作一個小販，在街上過日子，叫著：「鐲子呀，亮晶晶的鐲子！」

下午四點，我從學校回家。

從家門口，我看得見一個園丁在那裡掘地。

他用他的鋤子，要怎麼掘，便怎麼掘，他被塵土汙了衣裳，如果他被太陽曬黑了或是身上被打濕了，都沒有人罵他。

我願意我是一個園丁，在花園裡掘地。誰也不來阻止我。

天色剛黑，媽媽就送我上床。

從開著的窗口，我看得見更夫走來走去。

小巷又黑又冷清，路燈立在那裡，像頭上生著一隻紅眼睛的巨人。

VOCATION

When the gong sounds ten in the morning and I walk to school by
our lane,

Every day I meet the hawker crying, "Bangles, crystal bangles!"

There is nothing to hurry him on, there is no road he must take, no
place he must go to, no time when he must come home.

I wish I were a hawker, spending my day in the road, crying, "Bangles,
crystal bangles!"

When at four in the afternoon I come back from the school,

I can see through the gate of that house the gardener digging the
ground.

He does what he likes with his spade, he soils his clothes with dust,
nobody takes him to task if he gets baked in the sun or gets wet.

I wish I were a gardener digging away at the garden with nobody to
stop me from digging.

Just as it gets dark in the evening and my mother sends me to bed,

I can see through my open window the watchman walking up and
down.

更夫搖著他的提燈，跟他身邊的影子一起走著，他一生沒有一次上床去過。

我願是一個更夫，整夜在街上走，提著燈去追逐影子。

The lane is dark and lonely, and the street-lamp stands like a giant with one red eye in its head.

The watchman swings his lantern and walks with his shadow at his side, and never once goes to bed in his life.

I wish I were a watchman walking the streets all night, chasing the shadows with my lantern.

我做雲，你做月亮⋯⋯

我是波浪，你是陌生的岸⋯⋯

世界上就沒有一個人會知道我倆在什麼地方．

I shall be the cloud and you the moon.

I will be the waves and you will be a strange shore.

And no one in the world will know where we both are.

他沒有什麼事急著要做，他沒有哪條街一定要走，
他沒有什麼地方一定要去，他沒有什麼時間一定要回家．
There is nothing to hurry him on, there is no road he must take, no
place he must go to, no time when he must come home.

長者

媽媽，妳的孩子真傻！她是那麼可笑地不懂事！

她不知道路燈和星星的分別。

當我們玩著把小石子當食物的遊戲時，她以為那真是吃的東西，竟想放進嘴裡去。

當我翻開一本書，放在她面前，讓她讀 a，b，c 時，她卻用手把書頁撕了，無端快活地叫起來，妳的孩子就是這樣做功課的。

當我生氣地對她搖頭，罵她，說她頑皮時，她卻哈哈大笑，以為很有趣。

誰都知道爸爸不在家，但是，如果我在遊戲時高聲叫一聲「爸爸」，她便高興地四面張望，以為爸爸真是近在身邊。

當我把洗衣人帶來載衣服回去的驢子當做學生，並且告誡她，我是老師時，她卻無緣無故亂叫起我哥哥來。

妳的孩子要捉月亮。

她是這樣的可笑；她把格尼許 5 喚作琪奴許。

媽媽，妳的孩子真傻，她是那麼可笑地不懂事！

5　格尼許（ganesh）是毀滅之神濕婆的兒子，象頭人身。同時也是現代印度人所最喜歡用來做名字的第一個字。

SUPERIOR

Mother, your baby is silly! She is so absurdly childish!

She does not know the difference between the lights in the streets and the stars.

When we play at eating with pebbles, she thinks they are real food, and tries to put them into her mouth.

When I open a book before her and ask her to learn her a, b, c, she tears the leaves with her hands and roars for joy at nothing; this is your baby's way of doing her lesson.

When I shake my head at her in anger and scold her and call her naughty, she laughs and thinks it great fun.

Everybody knows that father is away, but if in play I call aloud "Father," she looks about her in excitement and thinks that father is near.

When I hold my class with the donkeys that our washerman brings to carry away the clothes and I warn her that I am the schoolmaster, she will scream for no reason and call me dâdâ.

Your baby wants to catch the moon. She is so funny; she calls Ganesh Gânush.

Mother, your baby is silly, she is so absurdly childish!

小大人

我人很小，因為我是一個小孩子，等到我像爸爸一樣年紀時，便要變大了。

我的老師要是走來說道：「時候晚了，把你的石板，你的書拿來。」

我便要告訴他：「你不知道我已經同爸爸一樣大了嗎？我絕不再作什麼功課了。」

我的老師便將驚異地說道：「他讀書不讀書可以隨便，因為他是大人了。」

我將自己穿上衣裳，走到人群擁擠的市場裡去。

我的叔叔要是跑過來說道：「你要迷路了，我的孩子，讓我領著你吧。」

我便要回答：「你沒有看見嗎，叔叔，我已經同爸爸一樣大了？我決定要獨自一個人到市場裡去。」

叔叔便將說道：「是的，他隨便到哪裡去都可以，因為他是大人了。」

當我正拿錢給保姆時，媽媽便要從浴室中出來，我知道怎樣用鑰匙開銀箱。

媽媽要是說道：「你在做什麼呀，頑皮的孩子？」

我便要告訴她：「媽媽，妳不知道我已經同爸爸一樣大了嗎？

THE LITTLE BIG MAN

I am small because I am a little child. I shall be big when I am as old as my father is.

My teacher will come and say, "It is late, bring your slate and your books."

I shall tell him, "Do you not know I am as big as father? And I must not have lessons any more."

My master will wonder and say, "He can leave his books if he likes, for he is grown up."

I shall dress myself and walk to the fair where the crowd is thick.

My uncle will come rushing up to me and say, "You will get lost, my boy; let me carry you."

I shall answer, "Can't you see, uncle, I am as big as father. I must go to the fair alone."

Uncle will say, "Yes, he can go wherever he likes, for he is grown up."

Mother will come from her bath when I am giving money to my nurse, for I shall know how to open the box with my key.

Mother will say, "What are you about, naughty child?"

I shall tell her, "Mother, don't you know, I am as big as father, and I must give silver to my nurse."

Mother will say to herself, "He can give money to whom he likes, for he is grown up."

我必須拿錢給保姆。」

媽媽便將自言自語道：「他可以隨便把錢給他喜歡的人，因為他是大人了。」

當十月裡放假的時候，爸爸將要回家，他會以為我還是一個小孩子，為我從城裡帶了小鞋子和小綢衫來。

我便要說道：「爸爸，把這些東西給哥哥吧，因為我已經同你一樣大了。」

爸爸便將想了想，說道：「他可以隨便去買他自己穿的衣裳，因為他是大人了。」

In the holiday time in October father will come home and, thinking that I am still a baby, will bring for me from the town little shoes and small silken frocks.

I shall say, "Father, give them to my dâdâ, for I am as big as you are."

Father will think and say, "He can buy his own clothes if he likes, for he is grown up."

十二點鐘

媽媽，我現在真不想做功課了。我整個早晨都在念書呢。

妳說，現在還不過是十二點鐘。假定不會晚過十二點吧；

難道妳不能把十二點鐘想像成下午嗎？

我能夠輕易地想像：現在太陽已經到那片稻田的邊緣上了，

老態龍鐘的漁婆正在池邊采擷香草作她的晚餐。

我閉上了眼就能想到，馬塔爾樹下的陰影是更深黑了，池塘

裡的水看來黑得發亮。

假如十二點鐘能夠在黑夜裡來到，為什麼黑夜不能在十二點

鐘的時候來到呢？

TWELVE O'CLOCK

Mother, I do want to leave off my lessons now. I have been at my book all the morning.

You say it is only twelve o'clock. Suppose it isn't any later; can't you ever think it is afternoon when it is only twelve o'clock?

I can easily imagine now that the sun has reached the edge of that rice-field, and the old fisher-woman is gathering herbs for her supper by the side of the pond.

I can just shut my eyes and think that the shadows are growing darker under the madar tree, and the water in the pond looks shiny black.

If twelve o'clock can come in the night, why can't the night come when it is twelve o'clock?

著作家

妳說爸爸寫了許多書，但我卻不懂得他寫的東西。

他整個黃昏讀書給妳聽，但妳真懂得他的意思嗎？

媽媽，妳跟我們說的故事，真是好聽呀！我很好奇，爸爸為什麼不能寫那樣的書呢？

難道他從來沒有從他自己的媽媽那裡聽過巨人、神仙和公主的故事嗎？

還是已經完全忘記了？

他常常耽誤了沐浴，你不得不走去叫他一百多次。

你總要等著候著，把他的菜熱著等他，但他忘了，還儘管寫下去。

爸爸老是以著書為遊戲。

如果我一走進爸爸房裡去遊戲，你就要走來叫道：「真是一個頑皮的孩子！」

如果我稍微出一點聲音，妳就要說：「你沒有看見你爸爸正在工作嗎？」

老是寫了又寫，有什麼趣味呢？

當我拿起爸爸的鋼筆或鉛筆，像他一模一樣地在他的書上寫著，a，b，c，d，e，f，g，h，i，——那時，妳為什麼跟我生氣呢，媽媽？

AUTHORSHIP

You say that father writes a lot of books, but what he writes I don't understand.

He was reading to you all the evening, but could you really make out what he meant?

What nice stories, mother, you can tell us! Why can't father write like that, I wonder?

Did he never hear from his own mother stories of giants and fairies and princesses?

Has he forgotten them all?

Often when he gets late for his bath you have to go and call him an hundred times.

You wait and keep his dishes warm for him, but he goes on writing and forgets.

Father always plays at making books.

If ever I go to play in father's room, you come and call me, "what a naughty child!"

If I make the slightest noise, you say, "Don't you see that father's at his work?"

What's the fun of always writing and writing?

When I take up father's pen or pencil and write upon his book just as he does,--a, b, c, d, e, f, g, h, i,--why do you get cross with me, then,

爸爸寫時，妳卻從來不說一句話。

當我爸爸耗費了那麼一大堆紙時，媽媽，妳似乎全不在乎。

但是，如果我只取了一張紙去做一艘船，妳卻要說：「孩子，你真討厭！」

妳對爸爸拿黑點子塗滿紙的兩面，汙損了許多許多張紙，心裡又是怎麼想的呢？

mother?

You never say a word when father writes.

When my father wastes such heaps of paper, mother, you don't seem to mind at all.

But if I take only one sheet to make a boat with, you say, "Child, how troublesome you are!"

What do you think of father's spoiling sheets and sheets of paper with black marks all over on both sides?

惡郵差

妳為什麼坐在地板上不言不動,告訴我呀,親愛的媽媽?

雨從開著的窗口打了進來,把妳身上全打濕了,妳卻不管。

妳聽見鐘已打了四下嗎?正是哥哥從學校裡回家的時候了。

到底發生了什麼事,妳的神色這樣不對?

妳今天沒有接到爸爸的信嗎?

我看見郵差在他的袋裡帶了許多信來,幾乎鎮裡的每個人都分送到了。

只有爸爸的信,他留起來給他自己看。我確信這個郵差是個壞人。

但是不要因此不樂呀,親愛的媽媽。

明天是鄰村市集的日子。妳叫女僕去買些筆和紙來。

我自己會寫爸爸所寫的一切信;妳找不出一點錯處來。

我要從字母 a 一直寫到 k。

但是,媽媽,妳為什麼笑呢?

妳不相信我能寫得同爸爸一樣好!

但是我會用心畫格子,把所有的字母都寫得又大又美。

當我寫好了,妳以為我也會像爸爸那樣傻,把它投入可怕的郵差袋中嗎?

THE WICKED POSTMAN

Why do you sit there on the floor so quiet and silent, tell me, mother dear?

The rain is coming in through the open window, making you all wet, and you don't mind it.

Do you hear the gong striking four? It is time for my brother to come home from school.

What has happened to you that you look so strange?

Haven't you got a letter from father to-day?

I saw the postman bringing letters in his bag for almost everybody in the town.

Only, father's letters he keeps to read himself. I am sure the postman is a wicked man.

But don't be unhappy about that, mother dear.

To-morrow is market day in the next village. You ask your maid to buy some pens and papers.

I myself will write all father's letters; you will not find a single mistake.

I shall write from A right up to K.

But, mother, why do you smile?

You don't believe that I can write as nicely as father does!

But I shall rule my paper carefully, and write all the letters beautifully big.

我立刻就自己送來給你，而且一個字母、一個字母地幫你讀。

我知道是那郵差不肯把真正的好信送給你。

When I finish my writing, do you think I shall be so foolish as father and drop it into the horrid postman's bag?

I shall bring it to you myself without waiting, and letter by letter help you to read my writing.

I know the postman does not like to give you the really nice letters.

英雄

媽媽，想像我們正在旅行，經過一個陌生而危險的國土。

妳坐在轎子裡，我騎著紅馬，在妳旁邊跑著。

是黃昏的時候，太陽已經下山。約拉地希的荒地疲乏而灰暗地展開在我們面前，大地淒涼而荒蕪。

妳害怕了，想著——「我不知道我們到了什麼地方。」

我對妳說道：「媽媽，不要害怕。」

草地上刺蓬蓬地長著針尖似的草，一條狹而崎嶇的小道通過這塊草地。

在這片廣大的地面上看不見一隻牛；它們已經回到村裡的牛棚去了。

天色黑了下來，大地和天空都顯得朦朦朧朧，而我們說不出正走向什麼所在。

突然間，妳叫我，悄悄問我：「靠近河岸的是什麼火光呀？」

正在那個時候，一陣可怕的吶喊聲爆發了，好些人影向我們跑來。

妳蹲坐在妳的轎子裡，嘴裡反覆禱念著神的名字。

轎夫們，怕得發抖，躲藏在荊棘叢中。

我向妳喊道：「不要害怕，媽媽，有我在這裡。」

他們手執長棒，披頭散髮，越走越近了。

226

THE HERO

Mother, let us imagine we are travelling, and passing through a strange and dangerous country.

You are riding in a palanquin and I am trotting by you on a redhorse.

It is evening and the sun goes down. The waste of Joradighi lies wan and grey before us. The land is desolate and barren.

You are frightened and thinking--"I know not where we have come to."

I say to you, "Mother, do not be afraid."

The meadow is prickly with spiky grass, and through it runs an arrow broken path.

There are no cattle to be seen in the wide field; they have gone to their village stalls.

It grows dark and dim on the land and sky, and we cannot tell where we are going.

Suddenly you call me and ask me in a whisper, "What light is that near the bank?"

Just then there bursts out a fearful yell, and figures come running towards us.

You sit crouched in your palanquin and repeat the names of the gods in prayer.

The bearers, shaking in terror, hide themselves in the thorny bush.

我喊道：「當心！你們這些壞蛋！再向前走一步，你們就要
送命了。」

他們又發出一陣可怕的吶喊聲，向前衝過來。

妳抓住我的手，說道：「好孩子，看在上天的份上，躲開他
們吧。」

我說道：「媽媽，妳瞧我的。」

於是我策馬猛奔，我的劍和盾彼此碰撞作響。

這場戰鬥是那麼激烈，媽媽，如果妳從轎子裡看得見的話，
妳一定會發顫的。

他們之中，許多人逃走了，還有好些人被砍殺了。

我知道妳那時獨自坐在那裡，心裡正在想著，妳的孩子這時
候一定已經死了。

但是我跑到妳跟前，渾身濺滿了鮮血，說道：「媽媽，現在
戰爭已經結束了。」

妳從轎子裡走出來，吻著我，把我摟在妳心頭，自言自語地
說道：

「如果沒有我的孩子護送我，我簡直不知道怎麼辦才好。」

上千件無聊的事天天在發生，為什麼這樣一件大事不能偶然
實現？

這樣一件很像書裡故事的一件大事。

我的哥哥會說：「這是可能的嗎？我老是在想，他是那麼嫩
弱呢！」

I shout to you, "Don't be afraid, mother. I am here."

With long sticks in their hands and hair all wild about their heads, they come nearer and nearer.

I shout, "Have a care! you villains! One step more and you are dead men."

They give another terrible yell and rush forward.

You clutch my hand and say, "Dear boy, for heaven's sake, keep away from them."

I say, "Mother, just you watch me."

Then I spur my horse for a wild gallop, and my sword and buckler clash against each other.

The fight becomes so fearful, mother, that it would give you a cold shudder could you see it from your palanquin.

Many of them fly, and a great number are cut to pieces.

I know you are thinking, sitting all by yourself, that your boy must be dead by this time.

But I come to you all stained with blood, and say, "Mother, the fight is over now."

You come out and kiss me, pressing me to your heart, and you say to yourself,

"I don't know what I should do if I hadn't my boy to escort me."

A thousand useless things happen day after day, and why couldn't such a thing come true by chance?

It would be like a story in a book.

我們村裡的人們都要驚訝道：「這孩子正和他媽媽在一起，
這不是很幸運嗎？」

My brother would say, "Is it possible? I always thought he was so delicate!"

Our village people would all say in amazement, "Was it not lucky that the boy was with his mother?"

告別

該是我離開的時候了，媽媽，我要走了。

當清寂的黎明，妳在暗中伸出雙臂，要抱妳睡在床上的孩子時，我要說道：「孩子不在那裡呀！」——媽媽，我走了。

我要變成一股清風撫摸妳；我要變成水的漣漪，當妳洗浴時，要把妳吻了又吻。

大風之夜，當雨點在樹葉中淅瀝時，妳在床上，會聽見我的低語，當電光從敞開的窗口閃進妳屋裡時，我的笑聲也偕了它一同閃進。

如果妳醒著躺在床上，想妳的孩子到深夜，我便要從星空向妳唱道：「睡呀！媽媽，睡呀。」

我要坐在各處游蕩的月光上，偷偷來到妳的床上，趁妳睡著時，躺在妳胸上。

我要變成一個夢，從妳眼皮的微縫中，鑽到妳睡眠的深處。當妳醒來吃驚地四望時，我便如閃耀的螢火蟲熠熠地向暗中飛去了。

當普耶節日[6]，鄰舍家的孩子們來屋裡遊玩時，我便要融化在

---

6 普耶（puja），意為「祭神大典」，這裡的「普耶節」，是指印度十月間的「難近母祭日」。

THE END

It is time for me to go, mother; I am going.

When in the paling darkness of the lonely dawn you stretch out your arms for your baby in the bed, I shall say, "Baby is not there!"--mother, I am going.

I shall become a delicate draught of air and caress you; and I shall be ripples in the water when you bathe, and kiss you and kiss you again.

In the gusty night when the rain patters on the leaves you will hear my whisper in your bed, and my laughter will flash with the lightning through the open window into your room.

If you lie awake, thinking of your baby till late into the night, I shall sing to you from the stars, "Sleep mother, sleep."

On the straying moonbeams I shall steal over your bed, and lie upon your bosom while you sleep.

I shall become a dream, and through the little opening of your eyelids I shall slip into the depths of your sleep; and when you wake up and look round startled, like a twinkling firefly I shall flit out into the darkness.

When, on the great festival of _puja_, the neighbours' children come and play about the house, I shall melt into the music of the flute and throb in your heart all day.

Dear auntie will come with puja-presents and will ask, "Where is our

笛聲裡，整日價在妳心頭震蕩。

親愛的阿姨帶了普耶禮[7]來，問道：「我們的孩子在哪裡，姊姊？」媽媽，妳將要柔聲告訴她：「他呀，他在我的瞳仁裡，在我的身體裡，在我的靈魂裡。」

---

baby, sister? Mother, you will tell her softly, "He is in the pupils of my eyes, he is in my body and in my soul."

召喚

她走的時候，夜裡黑漆漆的，他們都睡了。

現在，夜裡也是黑漆漆的，我喚她：「回來，我的寶貝；世界都在沉睡，當星星互相凝視的時候，妳來一會兒沒有人會知道。」

她走的時候，樹木正在萌芽，春光剛剛來到。

現在花已盛開，我喚道：「回來，我的寶貝。孩子們漫不經心地在遊戲，把花聚在一起，又把它們散開。妳如走來，拿一朵小花去，沒有人會發現。」

常常在遊戲的那些人，仍然在那裡遊戲，生命總是如此浪費。

我靜聽他們的空談，便喚道：「回來，我的寶貝，媽媽的心裡充滿著愛，妳如走來，僅僅從她那裡接一個小小的吻，沒有人會妒忌。」

THE RECALL

The night was dark when she went away, and they slept.

The night is dark now, and I call for her, "Come back, my darling; the world is asleep; and no one would know, if you came for a moment while stars are gazing at stars."

She went away when the trees were in bud and the spring was young.

Now the flowers are in high bloom and I call, "Come back, my darling. The children gather and scatter flowers in reckless sport. And if you come and take one little blossom no one will miss it."

Those that used to play are playing still, so spendthrift is life.

I listen to their chatter and call, "Come back, my darling, for mother's heart is full to the brim with love, and if you come to snatch only one little kiss from her no one will grudge it."

第一次的茉莉

呵，這些茉莉花，這些白色茉莉花！

我依稀記得我第一次雙手滿捧這些茉莉花，這些白色茉莉花
之時。

我喜愛那日光，那天空，那綠色的大地；

我聽見那河水淙淙的流動，在黑漆的午夜裡傳過來；

秋天的夕陽，在荒原上大路轉角處迎我，如新婦揭起她的面
紗迎接她的愛人。

但我想起孩提時第一次捧在手裡的白茉莉，心裡充滿甜蜜的
回憶。

我生平有過許多快活的日子，在節日宴會的晚上，我曾跟著
說笑話的人大笑。

在灰暗的雨天的早晨，我吟哦過許多飄逸的詩篇。

我頸上戴過愛人手織的醉花圈，作為晚裝。

但我想起孩提時第一次捧在手裡的白茉莉，心裡充滿甜蜜的
回憶。

THE FIRST JASMINES

Ah, these jasmines, these white jasmines!

I seem to remember the first day when I filled my hands with these jasmines, these white jasmines.

I have loved the sunlight, the sky and the green earth;

I have heard the liquid murmur of the river through the darkness of midnight;

Autumn sunsets have come to me at the bend of a road in the lonely waste, like a bride raising her veil to accept her lover.

Yet my memory is still sweet with the first white jasmines that I held in my hand when I was a child.

Many a glad day has come in my life, and I have laughed with merrymakers on festival nights.

On grey mornings of rain I have crooned many an idle song.

I have worn round my neck the evening wreath of bakulas woven by the hand of love.

Yet my heart is sweet with the memory of the first fresh jasmines that filled my hands when I was a child.

榕樹

喂，站在池邊的蓬頭的榕樹，你可會忘記那些小小的孩子，
就像忘記那些在你枝上築巢又離開你的鳥兒？

你不記得是他如何坐在窗內，詫異地望著你深入地下糾纏的
樹根嗎？

婦人們常到池邊，汲了滿罐的水去，你巨大的黑影便在水面
上搖動，好像睡著的人掙扎著要醒來。

日光在微波上跳舞，好像不停不息的梭子織著金色的花毯。

兩隻鴨子挨著蘆葦，在蘆葦影子上游來游去，孩子靜靜坐在
那裡想著。

他想成為風，吹過你蕭蕭的枝椏；想做你的影子，在水面上，
隨著日光俱長；想做一隻鳥兒，棲息在你的最高枝上；還想
成為那兩隻鴨，在蘆葦與陰影間游來遊去。

THE BANYAN TREE

O you shaggy-headed banyan tree standing on the bank of the pond, have you forgotten the little child, like the birds that have nested in your branches and left you?

Do you not remember how he sat at the window and wondered at the tangle of your roots that plunged underground?

The women would come to fill their jars in the pond, and your huge black shadow would wriggle on the water like sleep struggling to wake up.

Sunlight danced on the ripples like restless tiny shuttles weaving golden tapestry.

Two ducks swam by the weedy margin above their shadows, and the child would sit still and think.

He longed to be the wind and blow through your rustling branches, to be your shadow and lengthen with the day on the water, to be a bird and perch on your top-most twig, and to float like those ducks among the weeds and shadows.

祝福

祝福這個小小心靈，這個潔白的靈魂，他為我們的大地，贏得了天空的親吻。

他愛日光，他愛看媽媽的臉。

他沒有學會厭惡塵土而渴求黃金。

緊抱他在你的心裡，並且祝福他。

他已來到這個歧路百出的大地上了。

我不知道他怎麼從群眾中選出你來，來到你的門前抓住你的手問路。

他笑著，說著，跟著你走，心裡沒有一點疑惑。

不要辜負他的信任，引導他到正路，並且祝福他。

把你的手按在他的頭上，祈求著：底下的波濤雖然險惡，然而上面吹來的風，會鼓起他的船帆，送他到和平的港口。

不要在忙碌中把他忘了，讓他來到你的心裡，並且祝福他。

BENEDICTION

Bless this little heart, this white soul that has won the kiss of heaven for our earth.

He loves the light of the sun, he loves the sight of his mother's face.

He has not learned to despise the dust, and to hanker after gold.

Clasp him to your heart and bless him.

He has come into this land of an hundred cross-roads.

I know not how he chose you from the crowd, came to your door, and grasped your hand to ask his way.

He will follow you, laughing and talking, and not a doubt in his heart.

Keep his trust, lead him straight and bless him.

Lay your hand on his head, and pray that though the waves underneath grow threatening, yet the breath from above may come and fill his sails and waft him to the haven of peace.

Forget him not in your hurry, let him come to your heart and bless him.

贈禮

我要送些東西給你，我的孩子，因為我們同樣漂泊在世界的
溪流中。

我們的生活將被分離，我們的愛也將被遺忘。

但我卻沒有那樣傻，奢求能用我的贈禮來收買你的心。

你的生命正值青春，你的道路也長著，你一口氣飲盡我們給
你的愛，便回身離開我們跑了。

你有你的遊戲，有你的遊伴。如果你沒有時間同我們在一起，
如果你想不起我們，又能有什麼傷害呢？

我們呢，自然的，在老年時，會有許多閒暇的時間，去計算
那過去的日子，把我們手裡永遠失去的東西，在心裡愛撫著。

河流唱著歌很快地流去，沖破所有堤防。但是山峰卻留在那
裡，憶念著，滿懷依依之情。

THE GIFT

I want to give you something, my child, for we are drifting in the
stream of the world.

Our lives will be carried apart, and our love forgotten.

But I am not so foolish as to hope that I could buy your heart with my
gifts.

Young is your life, your path long, and you drink the love webring you
at one draught and turn and run away from us.

You have your play and your playmates. What harm is there if you
have no time or thought for us.

We, indeed, have leisure enough in old age to count the days that are
past, to cherish in our hearts what our hands have lost forever.

The river runs swift with a song, breaking through all barriers.

But the mountain stays and remembers, and follows her with his love.

我的歌

我的孩子，我這首歌將揚起樂聲圍繞在你的身旁，像那愛情熱戀的手臂一樣。

我這首歌將觸著你的前額，像那祝福的親吻一樣。

當你獨自一人時，它將坐在你的身旁，在你耳邊微語；當你身處人群中央，它將圈住你，使你超然物外。

我的歌將成為你夢的雙翼，它將把你的心移送到不可知的岸邊。

當黑夜覆蓋你的道路時，它又將成為那照臨在你頭上的忠實星光。

我的歌又將坐在你眼睛的瞳仁裡，將你的視線帶入萬物心裡。

當我的聲音因死亡而沉寂時，我的歌仍將在你跳動的心中唱著。

MY SONG

This song of mine will wind its music around you, my child, like the fond arms of love.

This song of mine will touch your forehead like a kiss of blessing.

When you are alone it will sit by your side and whisper in your ear, when you are in the crowd it will fence you about with aloofness.

My song will be like a pair of wings to your dreams, it will transport your heart to the verge of the unknown.

It will be like the faithful star overhead when dark night is over your road.

My song will sit in the pupils of your eyes, and will carry your sight into the heart of things.

And when my voice is silent in death, my song will speak in your living heart.

孩子天使

他們喧嘩爭鬥，他們懷疑失望，他們辯論而沒有結果。

我的孩子，讓你的生命到他們當中去，如一線鎮定而純潔的光芒，使他們愉悅而沉默。

他們的貪心和妒忌是殘忍的；他們的話，像暗藏的刀，渴望飲血。

我的孩子，去，去站在他們憤懣的心中，把你和善的眼光落在它們上面，像傍晚寬宏大量的和平，覆蓋日間的騷擾一樣。

我的孩子，讓他們望著你的臉，因此得知一切事物的意義；讓他們愛你，因此他們能夠相愛。

來，坐在無垠的胸膛上，我的孩子。朝陽出來時，開放而且抬起你的心，像一朵盛開的花；夕陽落下時，低下你的頭，默默做完這一天的禮拜。

THE CHILD-ANGEL

They clamour and fight, they doubt and despair, they know no end to their wranglings.

Let your life come amongst them like a flame of light, my child, unflickering and pure, and delight them into silence.

They are cruel in their greed and their envy, their words are like hidden knives thirsting for blood.

Go and stand amidst their scowling hearts, my child, and let your gentle eyes fall upon them like the forgiving peace of the evening over the strife of the day.

Let them see your face, my child, and thus know the meaning of all things; let them love you and thus love each other.

Come and take your seat in the bosom of the limitless, my child.

At sunrise open and raise your heart like a blossoming flower, and at sunset bend your head and in silence complete the worship of the day.

最後的買賣

早晨，我走在鋪著石子的路上，叫道：「誰來雇用我呀。」

皇帝坐著馬車，手裡拿著劍走來。

他拉著我的手，說道：「我要用權力來雇用你。」

但是他的權力算不了什麼，於是他坐著馬車走了。

正午炎熱的時候，家家戶戶的門都閉著。

我沿著曲折的小巷走去。

一個老人帶著一袋金幣走出來。

他斟酌了一會兒，說道：「我要用金幣來雇用你。」

他一個一個地數著他的錢幣，我卻轉身離去。

黃昏時，花園的籬上滿開著花。

美人走出來，說道：「我要用微笑來雇用你。」

她的微笑黯淡了，化成淚容，她孤寂地回身走進黑暗裡。

太陽照耀在沙地上，海波任性地四濺浪花。

一個孩子坐在那裡玩貝殼。

他抬起頭來，好像認識我似的，說道：「我雇你不用任何東西。」

從此以後，在這個孩子遊戲中做成的買賣，使我成了一個自由的人。

THE LAST BARGAIN

"Come and hire me," I cried, while in the morning I was walking on the stone-paved road.

Sword in hand, the King came in his chariot.

He held my hand and said, "I will hire you with my power."

But his power counted for nought, and he went away in his chariot.

In the heat of the midday the houses stood with shut doors.

I wandered along the crooked lane.

An old man came out with his bag of gold.

He pondered and said, "I will hire you with my money."

He weighed his coins one by one, but I turned away.

It was evening. The garden hedge was all a flower.

The fair maid came out and said, "I will hire you with a smile."

Her smile paled and melted into tears, and she went back alone into the dark.

The sun glistened on the sand, and the sea waves broke waywardly.

A child sat playing with shells.

He raised his head and seemed to know me, and said, "I hire you with nothing."

From thenceforward that bargain struck in child's play made me a free man.

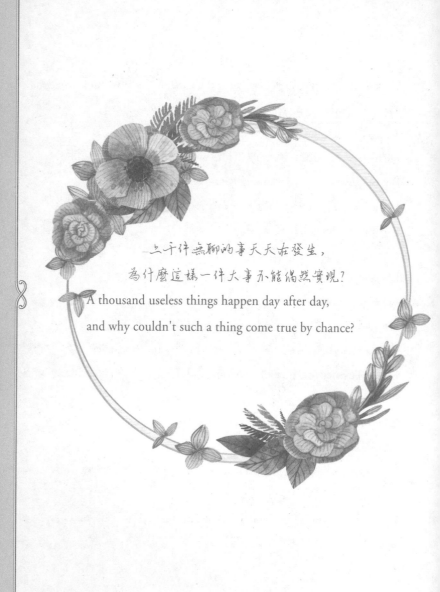

一千件無聊的事天天在發生，

為什麼這樣一件大事不能偶然實現？

A thousand useless things happen day after day,

and why couldn't such a thing come true by chance?

本書圖片來源

國家圖書館出版品預行編目 (CIP) 資料

生如夏花：泰戈爾新月漂鳥集：復刻印度名家彩
色插畫 譯者導讀泰戈爾生平與作品 / 泰戈爾
(Rabindranath Tagore) 著；鄭振鐸譯. -- 初版. -- 新北
市：野人文化出版：遠足文化發行, 2018.08
　面；　公分. -- (Golden age；33)
中英對照
ISBN 978-986-384-292-7(精裝)

867.51　　　　　　　　　　　　　107010513

生如夏花・泰戈爾新月漂鳥集

線上讀者回函專用 QR CODE，您的
寶貴意見，將是我們進步的最大動力。

Golden Age 33

生如夏花・泰戈爾新月漂鳥集【中英對照｜絕美精裝版】
復刻印度名家彩色插畫｜譯者導讀泰戈爾生平與作品
Stray Birds & The Crescent Moon

作　　者　泰戈爾 Rabindranath Tagore
譯　　者　鄭振鐸

社　　長　張瑩瑩
總 編 輯　蔡麗真
責任編輯　徐子涵
行銷企劃　林麗紅
封面設計　井十二設計研究室
內頁排版　洪素貞

出　　版　野人文化股份有限公司
發　　行　遠足文化事業股份有限公司（讀書共和國出版集團）
　　　　　地址：231 新北市新店區民權路 108-2 號 9 樓
　　　　　電話：（02）2218-1417　傳真：（02）8667-1065
　　　　　電子信箱：service@bookrep.com.tw
　　　　　網址：www.bookrep.com.tw
　　　　　郵撥帳號：19504465 遠足文化事業股份有限公司
　　　　　客服專線：0800-221-029
法律顧問　華洋法律事務所 蘇文生律師
印　　製　成陽印刷股份有限公司
初　　版　2018 年 10 月
初版16刷　2023 年 8 月

野人文化
讀者回函卡

書　名 _____

姓　名 _____ □女 □男　年齡 _____

地　址 _____

_____

電　話 _____　手機 _____

Email _____

□同意 □不同意　　收到野人文化新書電子報

學　歷 □國中(含以下) □高中職　　□大專　　　□研究所以上
職　業 □生產/製造　□金融/商業　□傳播/廣告　□軍警/公務員
　　　　□教育/文化　□旅遊/運輸　□醫療/保健　□仲介/服務
　　　　□學生　　　　□自由/家管　□其他

◆你從何處知道此書？
□書店：名稱 _____　　□網路：名稱 _____
□量販店：名稱 _____　　□其他 _____

◆你以何種方式購買本書？
□誠品書店　□誠品網路書店　□金石堂書店　□金石堂網路書店
□博客來網路書店　□其他 _____

◆你的閱讀習慣：
□親子教養　□文學 □翻譯小說 □日文小說 □華文小說 □藝術設計
□人文社科　□自然科學　□商業理財　□宗教哲學　□心理勵志
□休閒生活（旅遊、瘦身、美容、園藝等）　□手工藝／DIY　□飲食／食譜
□健康養生　□兩性 □圖文書／漫畫 □其他 _____

◆你對本書的評價：（請填代號，1.非常滿意　2.滿意　3.尚可　4.待改進）
書名 _____ 封面設計 _____ 版面編排 _____ 印刷 _____ 內容 _____
整體評價 _____

◆你對本書的建議：
_____

_____

_____

野人文化部落格 http://yeren.pixnet.net/blog
野人文化粉絲專頁 http://www.facebook.com/yerenpublish

請沿線撕下對折寄回

野人

書號：0NGA1033

Extended Reading
延伸閱讀

《先知》————————————————— The Prophet
卡里‧紀伯倫 | Kahlil Gibran | 著

西方世界一致譽為「小聖經」的崇高生命頌詩，黎巴嫩詩哲紀伯倫，綻放愛與真理之美的不朽散文詩集，深刻啟發披頭四、甘地、羅丹、冰心等中外名家。

《少年維特的煩惱》————————— Die Leiden des jungen Werther
約翰‧沃夫岡‧馮‧歌德 | Johann Wolfgang von Goethe | 著

維特是一個嚮往自由的年輕人，他多愁善感、直率可愛、熾熱激情。在一場舞會上，他與夏珞特相逢，對她一見鍾情。然而夏珞特已有婚約在身，深愛著未婚夫阿爾伯特。
這份暗戀將維特推向生命的極限，他體驗了極致的喜悅、極致的孤獨，然後是極致的絕望。他在愛中苦苦掙扎，同時又感受到自己與保守虛偽的封建社會格格不入。當悲痛超越了精神上的承受極限時，欲自救又不得解脫，他只剩毀滅一途。最終，維特抱著「為愛而死」的信念，飲彈自殺⋯⋯